"Big themes, strong characters, skillful world-building, suspenseful storytelling, witty dialogue, and even a dash of romance — [*The Killing of Bere Baudin*] checked all of the key boxes for me."

– Elizabeth Bruce
Senior Editor, Kevin Anderson
& Associates, New York City

See page 111 for a
news release about this book

.

THE KILLING OF BERE BAUDIN

THE KILLING OF BERE BAUDIN

A Dystopian Novel

DAVID DEMERS

MARQUETTE BOOKS LLC

PHOENIX, ARIZONA

LIBRARY OF CONGRESS CONTROL NUMBER
2022930985

ISBN for this print edition: 978-1-7327197-8-1
ISBN for the e-book edition: 978-1-7327197-7-4

Distributed by Ingram Book Company
Cover illustration by Jim Beihl
Interior design by Marquette Books

Published by

MARQUETTE BOOKS LLC
16421 North 31st Avenue
Phoenix, Arizona 85053
509-290-9240 (voice and text)
books@marquettebooks.com
https://MarquetteBooks.com

Also visit https://www.Luminars.org for updates

Author's Note

Iwrote this book not just to entertain, but to awaken.

The Killing of Bere Baudin portrays life four decades from now, in an America that has replaced democracy with Trumptocracy, an autocratic form of government. A dictator and 27 private corporations control the schools, government, police, and courts. Everything has been privatized. There is no "public," no voting, no free press, no due process, few environmental controls.

Although this book is a work of fiction, the notion that the United States or other democracies could embrace autocratic forms of rule is no longer in the exclusive realm of science fiction. Freedom House — a nonpartisan, nonprofit organization — has documented a 7 percent decline in democratic processes from 2017 to 2021, when Donald Trump was president.[1]

This book is not a prediction of what will come, but a warning of what could happen if Americans fail to defend democratic processes, civil liberties and due process. *–DD (January 2022)*

---

[1] This decline is interpolated from data in Sarah Repucci and Amy Slipowitz, "Democracy Under Siege," *Freedom in the World 2021* (New York: Freedom House, 2021), p. 10, retrieved Dec. 29, 2021, from <https://freedomhouse.org/report/freedom-world/2021/democracy-under-siege> and other Freedom House reports. The study found that democratic processes in America declined 11 percent from 2010 to 2020.

Glossary

Political Groups
> *Trumpians* — Conservatives obsessed with wealth, power, status
> *Luminars* — Progressives fighting to restore democracy, freedom, due process, free speech

Social Classes (Ordered from top to bottom)
> *Gebieter* — Supreme leaders for life (selected by the Lineals)
> *Lineals* — CEOs of 27 corporations who select/advise the Gebieter
> *Vorsters* — Upper-level corporate executives
> *Verwalters* — Low-level corporate managers
> *Klugs* — The professional class (engineers, technocrats, teachers)
> *Paysans* — Laborers, working class
> *Dregs* — Unemployed, lawbreakers, political prisoners

Partitions (in and around the City of Phoenix)
> 3 A wall-less prison surrounded by a powerful invisible electric fence. Governed by gangs and militia groups. The chronic unemployed and individuals convicted of civil and political crimes (including associating with Luminars) forced to live here.
> 2 The Verwalters, Klugs and Paysans live here, a middle-class area that separates partitions 1 and 3.
> 1 A secured area, formerly known as Paradise Valley. The Gebieter, Lineals, Vorsters live here, under a dome of fresh air.

Meaning of Names
> Baudin — Bold, brave (French)
> Bere — Courage (alternate spelling of bear)
> Kiryn — Beam or ball of light (Indian)
> Zach — God has remembered (Hebrew)
> Sara — Princess/Lady (Hebrew)
> Claire — Bright/Luminous (French)
> Bryce — Swift (Celtic)
> Otto — Wealthy (German)
> Heidi — Nobility (German)
> Rodriguez — Renown, power (Spanish)

1

The musty-sweet odor of concrete irritates my nostrils as I wait for the elevator doors in the parking garage to open.

"Mr. Greenstone?" I ask each time a man emerges. I worry one of them will recognize me, even though the hood on my navy blue windbreaker covers most of my face.

On the fifth opening, a stocky forty-something man dressed in a gray seersucker suit, bolo tie, and cowboy hat responds, "Yes?"

I pause until the three women who rode the elevator with him are out of earshot.

"I'm Bere Baudin," I whisper, lowering the hood.

His broad face is expressionless, so I assume he doesn't recognize me.

"What can I do for you, Mr. Baudin?"

My heart is pounding so hard I can feel it in my fingertips. I draw a deep breath. "I — I want you to kill me."

Greenstone stiffens his posture. "You what?"

I glance around to see if anyone heard him. "Would you kill me, please?"

He shrugs. "I'm sorry. You have the wrong person. I'm a stockbroker, not a killer. But I can refer you to a good therapist."

I chuckle. "Sorry, I should have mentioned that my father, Bryce Baudin, referred me to you."

"The professor?"

I nod, relieved that he remembered my dad.

"How is he?" Greenstone asks.

"Missing."

"What?" Greenstone's brow furrows.

"My grandma and I haven't heard from him in a couple of days. But he gave me a message to give to you." I lean toward Greenstone and whisper in his ear, "'Man is born free, and everywhere he is in chains.' Now will you kill me, Mr. Greenstone?"

2

T hree Days Earlier
7:29 a.m., Friday, December 14, 2059
Phoenix, Arizona
Capital of the Trumpian States of America

My lips are inches away from kissing blue-eyed Heidi Schmidt — the smartest and third-prettiest girl in my sophomore class — when my alarm wakes me.

Dang it!

I've had a crush on Heidi since eighth grade, when we sat next to each other in science class. We talked about our friends and families. She told me about Booboo, a female Maltese, who slept next to her every night. Lucky dog. But now, since the start of the new school year, whenever I see her in the hallway, she just smiles and walks away. Sometimes I wonder if she still likes me.

"Bere, you getting ready for school?" my father calls into the hallway near my bedroom.

"I'm up, Dad. Thanks."

I sit up, wipe sleep crust from my eyes, and saunter

into my bathroom. The peach fuzz and a few patches of dark brown stubble on my chin and cheeks offer no resistance to my new Shillett Laser Razor. Sometimes I worry my beard won't fill in.

I insert a u-shaped oral tray that the Cresgate Corporation says is guaranteed to eliminate bad breath. The device whirs as its lasers clean, floss and whiten my teeth in less than thirty seconds.

"When I was your age," my father once told me, "I had to do all of this manually."

So glad I live in modern times. Grammy even remembers a time when people were fitted with dentures after their teeth fell out. Everyone has implants now, except those who are poor or live in Partition 3 with the Dregs.

I shower, dress and check my holographic communicator for messages. One is from Zach Rodriguez, my best friend. "Hey, bro," he says as his image pops up about a foot away from my face. "I'll meet you at the game tonight. I'll find us some seats."

"That works," I respond. "I'll get us some food. Tacos okay?"

"You bet. Thanks."

Our team is playing the Scottsdale Vandals for the state championship. Totally cool.

Another dozen messages are from corporations trying to sell me stuff. "Tired of carrying your communicator or wearing c-glasses or contacts?" one advertisement inquires. "This holiday season ask for the gift that frees your hands — Appsung X, the first communicator implant. Safe. Painless. Easy to use."

Awesome. Goin' to ask Dad to get me one for Christmas.

I open my bedroom door to the tantalizing aroma of sizzling ostrich bacon and make my way to the kitchen. My short, Chinese-heritage grandmother is standing in front of the stove, holding a spatula. Her gentle smile melts my heart.

"Good morning, Grammy," I say, kissing her cheek. "Smells *delicioso*."

"Morning, honey," she says, flipping the bacon. "How'd you sleep?"

"Great. How 'bout you?"

"Almost seven hours. Not bad for an old lady."

"You're not old, Grammy. You're like that cast-iron skillet — tough and ageless."

"That's sweet of you, honey. But I think I'm becoming more like the bacon: fat and greasy."

I chuckle but quickly counter, "No way, Grammy. You're probably even tough enough to beat me up?"

"That's why you should always obey your Grandma," she shoots back, playfully shaking the spatula at me.

We're laughing as my father enters the kitchen and joins the ribbing. "Are you threatening your grandma again, Bere?"

"It's the other way around, Dad. She threatened to beat me with the spatula."

"Well, I'm sure you deserve it."

"Spoken like a true tyrant," I punch back.

"Well, if you haven't noticed, this ain't a democracy,

Son."

I roll my eyes; Grammy laughs; and Dad fakes a frown.

I help Grammy set the table and serve the food. I create a burrito, wrapping a flour tortilla in bacon, scrambled emu eggs, orange slices, and spicy salsa. Dad told me that, when he was a kid, he ate pork bacon and chicken eggs for breakfast. But pandemics killed off most of the pigs and chickens. The ones that survived were moved to hermetically sealed buildings. Only the wealthy can afford pork and chicken now.

"This is the last day of your semester, isn't it?" Dad asks.

"Yup," I mumble, after taking a large bite of my burrito. "And our football team is playing for the state championship tonight."

"Bere, you shouldn't talk when your mouth is full," Grammy softly chides.

I nod and swallow.

"Who are you playing?" he asks, sipping his coffee. Dad doesn't keep up with things at school. He's too busy teaching at the university. But I don't mind. He's spent a lot of time with me through the years, since my mother died.

Grammy pushes her plate to the end of the table. "Bryce, when are you coming home tonight?"

"I teach my last class at 4, so about five-thirty."

"Okay, I'll have dinner ready by six."

"You don't have to set a plate for me, Grammy. I'll get somethin' to eat at the game with Zach. I'll be home before midnight."

"How about 11?" my dad suggests.

"11:30?"

"Okay, but if you're late," he grins, "I'll give Grammy permission to beat you with that spatula."

*   *   *   *   *

I enter the garage, climb into my two-seat dark brown Genford electromagnetic pod and activate its synthetic computer with the command, "Hello, Henry."

"Where to, Mr. Bere?" it responds in a baritone voice.

"School, Henry."

The ceiling retracts and Henry rises 88 feet, high enough to clear trees and buildings. I can see the barren landscape of North Mountain, located behind our home. Only bursage grows there.

The pod quietly cruises at forty miles per hour to Joseph R. McCarthy High School eight miles away. The powder-blue sky is filled with orange-tinted clouds and hundreds of other pods traversing to various destinations at different heights in this city of 16 million.

On the streets below, workers who can't afford pods — Paysans — make their way to work mostly in robotic gasoline-powered automobiles that often get mired in traffic jams. Grammy told me there was an effort long ago to eliminate fuels like gasoline, but the oil companies shut it down to save jobs. Thank goodness for that.

But we're not rich. We don't live in Partition 1, where the wealthy live under a geodesic dome with fresh air. We live in Partition 2 with the Paysans and the Klugs, which include teachers like my dad, engineers, and low-level corporate managers. The air is so polluted that on most days we have to wear respirators outdoors.

"Turn on the news, Henry."

"Yes, Mr. Bere."

A small holographic screen appears two feet in front of me.

"And the air pollution index is extremely high again today," says a female weathercaster wearing a yellow dirndl dress. "Don't forget to wear your respirator if you're going outside. On the bright side, though, today's high is expected to reach 86 degrees. Over to you, Genny."

"Thanks, Marsha," Genny says, straightening her back, which increases the size of her bosom beneath a light pink blouse. "In local news — Arizona Corporate Police last night shot and killed five armed Luminars at a subversive training camp in a remote area of the Mogollon Rim. Eleven others were arrested. No police were killed or injured. Our Jason Swift is at the scene."

Gee, that's only about 80 miles from here.

"Thanks, Genny," he says while standing in front of a smoldering building surrounded by ponderosa pines. "I'm here with Colonel Max Wagner, who led the raid. Colonel, can you tell our viewers what the Luminars were doing here?"

The camera zooms in on the Colonel's face, which

has a deep scar in its right cheek. "They were teaching seditious ideas and combat skills to new recruits, Jason. And they were planning to attack the Capitol in Phoenix. The Luminars are a cancer in our society. And like a cancer, we must eliminate every cell. ... "

"Damn Luminars," I mutter.

"What did you say, Mr. Bere?" Henry asks.

"Nothing, Henry. Turn news off."

Seconds later Henry descends into the school parking lot.

I check the time: 8:58.

Yikes! I'm going to be late for class. I'll cut through the gym.

3

8:59 a.m., Gymnasium
Joseph R. McCarthy High School

I enter the gymnasium on the north side, where three upperclassmen are playing basketball. I recognize one of them: Otto Wagner, a star offensive lineman on the football team.

I walk quietly to avoid detection, but he sees me, stops bouncing the ball, and yells, "Greenie!"

A second later his companions are sprinting toward me like coyotes chasing a rabbit.

I bolt for the nearest hallway exit on the south side of the gym. With a half-court lead, I know I can make it, but a basketball crosses my path and I trip. My body is airborne for a split second before it slams into the waxed wooden floor. OUCH!

"Nice throw, Otto," cackles one of his minions, as Otto struts toward me. "You could be a professional bowler."

Otto kneels next to me and grins like a hunter after a kill. "Look at this carcass."

He grabs my right arm and jerks me to a standing

position.

"We should pummel him with dodge balls," advises the other sidekick, whose jet-black hair is greased back.

My mind races to come up with something clever to bust up this sadistic shindig. "Before you turn me into a target, Mr. Wagner, may I, ah, say something in my defense?"

He nods.

"Wouldn't it be more fun beating up on someone your own size?"

Otto's comrades laugh.

But Otto gives them a side-eye, which shuts them up. He scowls at me. "Whattaya doin' in our gym, chink?"

"I'm late for class and this was a shortcut. Sorry for interrupting your game. So, if you don't mind, I'll be on my way." I turn and take one step.

"I do mind, chink boy," Otto says, grabbing my shoulder.

His racist remark sets me off.

"Did you know that term is degrading?" I frown.

Otto ignores me. "What's your name, chink boy?"

"Bere."

He chuckles and folds his arms across his chest. "What the hell kind of name is that?"

"The one my parents gave me."

Otto's companions laugh again but Otto ignores them.

"You think that's funny, chink boy?"

"Can't say I'd use that line in a comedy routine, but your buddies seemed to like it."

Otto's cheeks turn pink. "Why, you smart-ass," he roars as his massive hands encircle my neck and effortlessly lift my 121-pound body a foot off the floor. I grasp his wrists to minimize the choking, but it's still hard to breathe.

Otto was right.

I was a smart-ass.

I've always been a bit irreverent, especially when I'm scared. I'm sure a shrink would tell me it's my way of coping with stress. But none of that matters right now, because nothing I could say or do is going to stop this inglorious hazing party. So I accept my fate, which now manifests itself in the stars floating around Otto's shaved head. Shit, I'm going to pass out.

"Put that boy down!" a girl behind me shouts.

"Who are you?" Otto bellows.

"Sara Nuechterlein, the vice principal's daughter."

"No, you aren't."

"Try me, Otto. I can have you tossed off the football team before tonight's game. Put him down — NOW!"

Otto releases his grip.

I fall to the floor, coughing and gasping for air. The stars dissipate and my eyes reveal that my savior is the size of a ballerina and has waist-length auburn hair. She's wearing black gym shorts and a goldenrod t-shirt emblazoned with a hawk, the school's mascot. I've never seen her before, but that's not unusual, because there are 9,000 kids in my high school.

Otto spits at me. "A girl saved you this time, chink boy," he says, walking away with his buzzard buddies.

"But next time I see your egg-roll head, you're gonna wish you'd never been born."

"Stick the egg roll up your fat butt," I want to yell, but don't. Grammy wouldn't approve.

"You okay?" my savior asks, offering a hand to help me up.

"Thanks," I reply, standing. I rub my neck. "Are you really the vice principal's daughter?"

"Of course not."

"How'd you know Otto would fall for it?"

"Guys like Otto are afraid of girls," she replies, gracefully placing her hands on her hips.

"How do ya know that?"

"Because he's a bully; all bullies are insecure."

"What about guys who are insecure and aren't bullies?"

Her fern-green eyes widen and she grins, exposing a dimple in each cheek. "They're the ones we smart girls date."

"Even those who still sleep with their teddy bears?"

She laughs. "You're funny, Bere. But I bet your humor gets you in trouble now and then."

"Only when I walk through gyms filled with bullies and courageous girls."

She shows her dimples again.

"How can I thank you?" I ask.

"You goin' to the game tonight?"

"Of course."

"But what about Otto?"

"One cracked nut doesn't spoil the whole snack," I

say, rubbing my neck. "I'm not missing the most important Hawks game of the year."

"Okay, buy me an ice cream cone after the game and we're even. Meet me at the concession stand."

"It's a date."

"Ah — well, I wouldn't call it a date. I have a boyfriend."

"Sorry — I — ah — I didn't really mean — ah — I meant we should just have an ice cream meet-up."

She giggles at my awkwardness. "No offense taken."

"I have to warn you, though," I say, regaining my composure. "I'm a very talented ice cream eater."

"Well, I certainly hope you're more skilled at that than you are negotiating with bullies."

*　*　*　*　*

I quietly open the door to my government class and tiptoe in, knowing full well that Ms. Gomez, my teacher, has eyes in the back of her head. But she's still going through the morning school announcements, so maybe she won't see me.

"You're late, Bere," she says, without even turning to look at me.

How does she do that?

"Sorry, Ms. Gomez. I was hung up in the gym."

Smirks emerge on the faces of several classmates who have a reputation for reveling in the misfortune of others. My dad says the Germans have a name for that: *schadenfreude.*

Many teachers would mark me tardy. But Ms. Gomez knows I'm a good student and that I like her class.

I sit in the back row, next to my buddy Zach, who has a big grin on his face until he sees me up close. "Your neck is red, bro," he whispers. "You okay?"

I nod.

"Please stand for the pledge," Ms. Gomez commands.

My 26 classmates and I comply, putting our right fists over our hearts: "I pledge allegiance, to the Flag, of the Trumpian States of America, and to the Polity, for which it stands, one Nation, under Gebieter, indivisible, with loyalty and duty for all."

"Thank you, class."

We sit as Ms. Gomez summarizes the day's lesson. This year, for the first time, she and all teachers are required to use the Appsung X communicator implant. She says she loves it because it's hands-free.

"Today we continue our discussion of the Second Civil War. Appsung, play video of the White House, July 4, 2035."

A 10-foot-wide holographic image appears in the air behind her. The former White House is in flames — a scene I've seen a hundred times before.

"On this day Luminars attacked the White House, killing the Gebieter, five dozen security personal, and eight members of the Trumpian Confederate Party of America. The military responded with massive force, attacking Luminar groups across the country. The TCP declared a nationwide curfew and then … "

I stop listening — not because I don't respect Ms.

Gomez. She's a great teacher. But I'm so tired of hearing the same lecture year after year. Why do government classes repeat the same story over and over? They seem to think we students are dumb.

I stare out the window at a dying saguaro. Two of its graying arms are sagging, as though it's trying to cushion its descent before being absorbed by mother earth. All of the saguaros in the Senora Desert are dying, according to the government, because of a fungus created and planted by the Luminars. They want to overthrow the TCP and create a collectivist state, where everyone is a robot. They are so evil.

I feel a bit guilty for flirting with Sara behind Heidi's back. But, hey, Heidi and I haven't even had a date, so why should I feel guilty? Besides, lately, I don't even know if she likes me.

"Bere?"

I turn my head toward Ms. Gomez. "Ahhh — yes?"

"Did you hear the question?"

"I guess I didn't."

Giggles pepper the room.

"Why did the TCP eliminate voting rights?"

That's an easy question. "Because people aren't smart enough."

"And you agree?" Ms. Gomez follows up.

"Well, who couldn't? Before the war, the two major political parties couldn't agree on anything. Everything was polarized. Government was chaotic. There was violence in the streets. But now we have order, stability, and — "

"No voting rights," interrupts Kiryn Baker, an honors student who often speaks up in class. "We've lost our right to choose our leaders."

Several students gasp, including me, because Kiryn is advocating chaos.

"People have plenty of choices," I retort, riding the wave of outrage. "They can decide to do well or not in school, go to college, choose a career, pick a spouse. Duty and obedience are more important than voting. Voting creates chaos."

"Voting gives people hope," she kicks back.

"To what end? So people can bicker and fight about everything?"

"Voting didn't create chaos, Bere. False news reports did that. People need to respect each other's opinions."

"The idea that the news is false is a false idea, created by the Luminars. *You* sound like a Luminar, Kiryn."

Several students snicker.

"I'm not a Luminar." She frowns and folds her chocolate-toned arms. "I'm a loyal American, just like you. It's not a question of whether people are smart enough to vote. It's a question of whether they deserve the right to govern themselves."

"You're a Luminar, all right," I retort. "I bet your parents are, too."

The room falls eerily silent, and I instantly regret my comments. But Kiryn doesn't seem to respect the state or her duty to it. How can someone so smart be so dumb?

"Okay, enough of that," Ms. Gomez scolds, looking at

me. I turn my eyes to the floor. "But the debate between Kiryn and Bere raises an important question for all of us: Is giving up the right to vote a price worth paying to reduce conflict and violence?"

"Of course," says Burt Cumberlin, whose father manages the dealership where my dad buys his pods. "It prevents tyranny of the majority."

A half dozen others agree.

No one supports Kiryn.

*   *   *   *   *

"What happened to you?" Zach asks me as we leave the room.

But before I can respond, Ms. Gomez calls out, "Bere, may I please see you for a second?"

Zach grins and whispers: "I'll wait in the hallway, you bad boy."

I stare at the floor as I walk toward her, hoping she'll take some pity on me. She tilts her head down and looks at me over her reading glasses.

"I realize that you and the rest of the class are very patriotic, but you could have been nicer to Kiryn. When you criticize a person but not their argument, you're committing a logical fallacy — an ad hominem attack. Next time, provide reasons why you don't think voting empowers people."

"You're right, Ms. Gomez. I went overboard. I'm sorry."

"Don't apologize to me — apologize to Kiryn."

"Yes, ma'am. I will."

"And one more thing." She reaches for a paper on her desk — the one I wrote about Joseph McCarthy for extra credit. Oh, crap, I must have screwed it up.

Her face is expressionless as she looks at the paper. "In all my years I've never seen a term paper like this."

"I'm sorry, Ms. Gomez, I worked hard on it but — "

"You have superb writing skills, Bere. Where did you learn to write like this?"

She drops the paper into my hands, which has a score of "10" in the top right corner.

"I guess I learned a lot from my dad. He's a professor and has edited a lot of my stuff through the years."

"You criticized McCarthy for falsely accusing people of being communists. How did you know about that?"

"My grandmother gave me a book about him. He wasn't as truthful as some of my teachers have claimed. But he was still a great man. I'm sure our high school wouldn't be named after him if that weren't the case."

"I suppose not," she says, raising her eyebrows. "But that's a debate for another time. Have you thought about a career in writing?"

"Not really. I wanna be a Vorster and live in Partition 1."

"Nothing wrong with aspiring to be a top-level executive. But maybe you can combine writing with something in management — maybe strategic communications." She smiles. "It was a pleasure having you in my class this semester, Bere. Have a wonderful holiday."

"Thanks. I will — and you too, Ms. Gomez."

I enter the hallway, which is bustling with students scurrying to their classes.

"What happened?" Zach asks.

"Ms. Gomez chewed me out for being mean to Kiryn and —— "

"Not that," Zach interrupts. "What happened in the gym?"

"Oh — Otto Wagner. He picked me up by my neck."

"Why?"

"Because he's an asshole."

"You gonna file a complaint?"

"What good would that do? Administrators only take action when a bully injures someone. Besides, Otto might make my life even more unbearable next semester. And I'd be cast as a wimp — which I am, of course, but don't tell anyone."

Zach chuckles. "That makes two of us, bro."

"But wimpiness has its advantages, dude — a cute girl saved me."

He grins. "Tell me more, bro."

"She told Otto she was the vice principal's daughter, and he released me when she threatened to have him suspended from the team."

"Wow, saved by a girl — and a cute girl."

"But there's only one problem."

"What's that?"

"She's got a boyfriend."

Zach's grin disappears and he scratches his head. "Well, seems to me there's only one solution to this problem, bro." He pauses. "You need to get Otto to beat you up again. After that, she'll be putty in your wimpy hands." He bursts out laughing.

I fake a stern look. "If you weren't my friend and I wasn't a wimp, I'd have you pinned on the floor right now."

"Thank goodness you're a wimp," he says.

"Gotta go, Zach. My chemistry teacher isn't as nice as Mrs. Gomez. See you tonight."

As we part, my mind turns to Kiryn. Ms. Gomez was right: It was wrong of me to accuse her and her parents of being Luminars. I need to apologize for that. But I'm right about self-governance. Voting produces nothing but chaos. Only corporate executives should rule — well, maybe some teachers, too. My dad's a good leader. But the laws would have to be changed for —

"Hey, Bere," a girl calls out, interrupting my thoughts and gait.

I stop and turn. "Heidi — hi — wow, you look great in that blue dress."

"Thanks," she says coyly. "You goin' to the game tonight, Bere?"

"Yeah. You?"

"Well, of course," she says, tilting her head back. "Like, maybe I'll see you there."

"I hope so."

She smiles and wraps a lock of her chest-length hair behind her left ear.

Wow, I wasn't sure she still liked me. Man, girls are hard to understand sometimes.

4

5:44 p.m., The Championship Game
McCarthy Indoor Football Stadium

"Hey, Bere. Up here."

Zach is waving at me from the upper section of the bleachers. He's surrounded by Hawks fans dressed in black and goldenrod t-shirts.

I nod instead of wave, because I'm carrying a tray of ostrich-steak tacos and power drinks. I look for Heidi as I climb the bleachers but don't see her.

"Oye, amigo," Zach says when I arrive. "Cómo estás?"

"Todavía estoy vivo," I reply with a heavy English accent.

We fist pump.

"So tell me more about this girl that saved you in the gym," he says, biting into a taco.

"Her name's Sara. Gorgeous auburn hair, down to her waist. I'm buying her an ice cream after the game."

"So maybe she's thinking about dumping her beau. Why else would she have asked you to buy her an ice cream?"

"Not everyone has an ulterior motive," I reply. "Besides, I'm not too upset about it. Heidi asked me whether I'd be at the game."

"Are you buying her an ice cream, too?" Zach ribs me. "Hey, maybe you could meet both of them after the game. It would save you some time."

I grin. "Well, at least I have a girl who wants to meet me."

"Hey, you're not the only Casanova around here," he says, biting into a taco. "Eleanor wants to meet me after the game."

"No kidding? That's great, dude."

"But who knows what she wants. Girls are hard to read."

"Tell me about it. Physics textbooks are easier to understand."

We chuckle and take another bite of our tacos.

The game begins, and for the next three hours Zach and I become part of the fanfare — screaming in joy when the Hawks move the ball down-field or score a touchdown; moaning in feigned pain when the accursed Scottsdale Vandals get the better of us. I keep looking for Heidi but don't see her.

The game is tied.

Two seconds left.

A fumble.

A Hawks player picks it up and powers past three Vandals to score a touchdown. Hawks fans jump to their feet and roar in triumph as the announcer says: "Ladies and gentlemen, that was Otto Wagner who scored the winning touchdown."

Why does the bully always get to be the hero? Why can't we wimpy guys win one once in a while?

"There's a party at Coyote Creek," Zach says as we climb down the bleachers. "Wanna go? Can I ride with you?"

"Sure. But I have to buy Sara an ice cream first."

"Can I meet her? I need to make sure she's good enough for you," he teases.

"Sure, Dad."

*　　*　　*　　*　　*

Most of the fans stay for a post game rally in the stadium.

Zach and I make our way down the bleachers but I still don't see Heidi.

We exit into the hallway and head toward the concession stand. Sara is standing next to it, leaning against the wall. She's wearing a teal knit sweater, plaid A-line skirt and loafers. She looks awesome, but I hold my compliment.

"Hi, Bere," she says, showing her dimples again. "Great game, eh?"

"Sure was. Sara, this is Zach Rodriguez, my best friend."

Zach's eyes are big. If he were a cartoon character, he'd be drooling.

"Nice to meet you, Zach," she says, gently shaking his hand.

33

"Nice to meet you, too."

"You know, Sara," I say, "I don't even know your last name."

"McMillan."

"That explains the red hair," Zach blurts out.

Sara giggles and I gently roll my eyes at Zach, who's blushing.

"It's okay," she quickly adds and smiles. "Zach is right. My father traces his roots to Scotland and my mother is Irish."

"I'm Swedish and Mexican," Zach says.

Sara and Zach are staring at me, waiting for my response. If I don't declare my ethnic heritage, we'll all feel awkward. "French and Chinese."

We find ourselves grinning uncomfortably until Zach saves the day. "Hey, I've got to find Eleanor. Nice meeting you, Sara."

"My pleasure, Zach."

"Meet me at my pod in a half hour," I say to Zach as he sprints away.

"Seems like a nice guy," Sara says.

"Yeah, he's all right as far as Swedes go," I say with a straight face.

She looks at me to see if I'm teasing, and then giggles.

"Zach is the best kind of best friend. He always has my back. Been that way since he lost his father and I lost my mother."

"I'm so sorry to hear that."

"A long time ago," I say, looking away from her in

case my eyes moisten. "Let's get some ice cream."

She orders a coffee ice cream cone and I order chocolate.

We exit the stadium on the south side of the building. I reach for my communicator, which falls out of my shirt pocket onto the sidewalk. This is when an Appsung X implant would be helpful, I tell myself. My communicator indicates the pollution level has dropped to moderate levels, so we don't need our respirators. It's warm out. We walk toward a concrete fence that separates the school property from a road.

"Did you see who scored the winning touchdown?" Sara asks, slowly licking the tip of her ice cream cone with her dainty pink tongue.

"Unfortunately, I did."

She laughs. "My dad once told me that life isn't fair, especially if you sit around and let it happen."

"Your dad sounds like a smart guy."

"He's a professor."

"Mine too. In what field?"

"Left field," she giggles. "Honestly, I can't understand what he's saying half the time. He's a geologist."

"Mine's an economist. Do you know why God created economists?"

"I sense a punch line coming," Sara says, licking her cone.

"In order to make weather forecasters look good."

She musters a laugh, which suggests to me that she's not the kind of person who shames people for bad jokes.

Our eyes briefly lock before I change subjects. "What's your favorite class?"

"Marketing. I wanna be a Vorster and live in Partition 1."

"Hey, me too — I mean I want to live in Partition 1," licking the side of my cone, which is dripping. "I'm just not sure what kind of Vorster I want to be. Ever been there?"

"Only once," she says, wiping a drip from her chin. "The dome is beautiful, isn't it? The air — so fresh, and it's so green in there. My dad was giving a lecture about the Superstitious Mountains." She looks up at the stars. "Did you know that some Apache Indians believe there's a hole in the mountains that leads straight to hell? They say that's where dust storms come from."

"That's probably where the Luminars live," I say, instantly regretting my comment.

Her forehead wrinkles. "You don't like Luminars?"

"Not especially."

"Do you know any?" she asks, licking the ice cream completely around the top of the cone's edge. My brain freezes for a second.

"Ah — ah — no, I guess not."

"Then how do you know you dislike them?" she asks.

I give her the textbook answer. "Because they started the Second Civil War."

"How do you know that?" She bites into the cone.

I divert my eyes to protect my thoughts. "Well, that's what I learned in school."

"Do you always believe what you hear in school?"

"No, but why would teachers and textbooks lie?"

She walks toward me and looks me directly in the eyes. "My dad always says that we shouldn't judge people until we walk in their shoes."

"But what if they have athlete's foot?" I say, trying to wiggle my way out of this debate.

She grins. "My dad would say that's even a better reason to walk in their shoes. Then you really understand their problems."

"So take your shoes off," I tease.

She looks at her feet. "My shoes are too small for your feet."

"Are you saying I have big feet?" I grin, confident I have taken the upper foot in this debate.

"No — I have small feet, and, besides, I only let boys try my shoes on during a second date." She dimples me.

I chuckle. "So," I pause for emphasis, "this is a date?"

"Did I just say that?" She giggles nervously. "I forgot that this was just an ice cream meet-up. My apologies."

"I'm not sure I want to forgive you," I say, feeling like a debater who has destroyed his foe's main argument. But before I can request another date, a powerful object hits my body and Sara screams, "BERE!"

My body slams into the gravelly ground. I can't breathe — wind knocked out of me. I raise my head, gasping desperately for air. The left side of my face is cold. Something wet is running down it. I catch a breath and open my eyes. Otto — of course — that bastard.

He grabs Sara's arm. She uses the other to throw her ice cream at him, which hits him in the forehead but has the same effect as an ice cube thrown into a large fire.

"Lemme go," she screams.

"You lied to me, bitch. I'm gonna teach you a lesson, and then I'm going to teach your chink boy a lesson." He tries to kiss her. She swings her left hand at his face, but his forearm deflects the blow.

I catch my breath and rise to my feet. "Hey, dimwit," I shout. "Why don't you pick on someone who's almost as ugly as you?"

Otto laughs, releases Sara, and walks toward me. His eyebrows are slanted toward the center of his face, and his hands out and cupped. He's hoping for a lead role in "Hang 'Em High 2."

"Run, Sara!" I shout. "Run!"

But she ignores me and yells at Otto. "Stop it! Leave Bere alone!"

I want to run, but I can't abandon Sara. So I stand my ground and defend myself the only way I know how: by thrusting my right knee upward, between Otto's log-sized legs.

He screams, grabs his crotch, and falls to his knees.

"You son of a bitch," he moans. "You kneed me."

"And you needed it, asshole."

He groans. "I'm — gonna — kill you!"

I dash toward Sara, whose eyes are humongous — like they needed more visual evidence to confirm what she just saw. "You just kneed him in the — "

"Wizzak," I interrupt. "Yup. But I think it's better if we leave now and talk about that later."

She nods once. We clasp hands and run as fast as we

can to the east side of the school; then north, toward the dying cactus I daydreamed about this morning. Did I really bring Otto to his knees? The whole thing was surreal. I look back. "I think we're in the clear," I say, trying to catch my breath.

We slow to a brisk walk near the front entrance of the school and giggle nervously about what just happened. A streetlight illuminates Sara's eyes, which are a deeper shade of green than when we met in the gym.

"Thanks, Bere," she says, still trying to catch her breath.

"Just returning the favor."

We stop and stare at each other for several seconds before I realize I'm still holding her hand. I release my grip and lower my eyes. "Sorry — forgot you have a boyfriend."

"I'm not entirely sure about that."

"Whattaya mean?"

"He stood me up tonight. He's out with his buddies."

"Is he ill?"

"What do you mean?"

"How can a bunch of buddies compare to you?"

She looks down at the ground. Did my flattering comment embarrass her?

A gasoline-powered car drives by and its fumes linger in the air.

Sara ignores the smell and touches my face, wiping ice cream off my face, which sends a tingle down my neck. "You know, if I didn't have a boyfriend, I'd hug you right now."

"And what would you do if your boyfriend were here?" I ask, wondering where I've been getting this courage to be so bold with a girl. I feel odd, yet strong.

She pulls my head toward hers and purses her coral-colored lips. I smell jasmine and close my eyes to enter paradise, but a brassy voice behind me pulls me back to earth.

"BEEERE! What are you doing?"

Sara releases my hand and the hairs on the back of my neck stand up.

"Ah — Heidi — hi — ah — "

"I didn't realize you had a girlfriend," she declares.

"I don't — this is Sara — a friend — Sara, this is Heidi."

My two potential girlfriends awkwardly nod at each other and then look at me. I'm frantically racking my brain for the right words to make everyone happy. But I can't find them.

"I'd better get going," Heidi says. "My friends are waiting."

"Wait, Heidi, I can explain."

"I thought you liked me," she sighs, as a mist forms over her dark brown eyes. One of her girlfriends, standing next to her, stares at me like a hunter looks down the barrel of a rifle. "Whatta scumbag. Let's get out of here, Heidi."

They turn and walk briskly away.

"Heidi, I can explain."

"Honestly, I don't want to hear it," she says, turning

her head back. "Leave me alone."

"I should go, Bere," Sara says, frowning.

"Wait, let me explain. Heidi and I aren't dating. In fact, we've rarely spoken to each other since last school year."

Sara ignores me and jogs toward the parking lot on the west side of the school.

I chase her. "Sara, wait. Please. Let me explain."

She stops, turns and stabs her left index finger into the air twice. "If you didn't have a relationship with Heidi, why did she get so upset? You may be good at eating ice cream and bringing down bullies, but you know nothing about relationships. I have to go. Leave me alone."

5

10:23 p.m., Parking Lot
Joseph R. McCarthy High School

In my sixteen long years, I cannot recall another day with more highs and lows.

A bully choked me; I insulted a smart girl; I flirted with two girls; I kicked the bully in the crotch; and I hurt the feelings of the two girls.

I need Zach.

I sprint to my pod, where he's standing, glued to his communicator. "Zach, you won't believe what just happened. I — "

"Sorry, Bere," he says, putting his communicator in his pocket. "Can't talk right now. Eleanor's waiting for me, over there, in her pod." He points and Eleanor waves. "She's taking me to the party. Is that okay? I'll see you there. We'll chat then."

"Yeah, no worries, bro. See you there."

But I lied.

I'm in no mood to party.

I climb into my pod.

"Home, Henry."

Henry comes to life but then shuts down.

"Someone is behind the pod, Mr. Bere."

I open the door, which rotates upward. I assume it's Zach. "What's up, dude?"

"No, it's Ms. Gomez, Bere," she says, coming into my line of sight.

"Oh, Ms. Gomez. I thought you were —— "

"Bere," she interrupts, dropping a ziphoid drive into my palm. "Take this. I don't have time to explain. Give it to your father as soon as you can. Don't tell anyone about this. This is extremely important. Do you understand?"

"I think so. But what's on it? What's going on?"

Ms. Gomez's eyes are bulging and her hands are shaking. "I don't have time to explain," she says, looking to her left and right. "But you must follow my directions. I've got to go before they see me."

"They? Who's 'they'?"

"Don't follow me, Bere, no matter what you see."

She runs and disappears behind a row of pods. I stare at the drive in my hand. I look around, but I see no one in the lot.

"Home Henry."

* * * * *

10:46 p.m.

Grammy is reading her communicator in the Arizona room when I arrive.

"Hi, honey," she says from her favorite chair, a

wooden rocker with the finish worn on the wooden arms. "You're back early."

I kiss her cheek. "Yeah, didn't feel like going out after the game." I want to tell her about the ziphoid drive, but Ms. Gomez's instructions were clear: speak to no one except my dad. I didn't even know Ms. Gomez knew him.

"Is Dad back?" I ask Grammy, who removes her reading glasses.

"No — probably got detained at work."

I turn to go to my room but pause and stare at a picture of the four of us — her, Dad, Mom and me — on the wall, trying to decide whether I should ask Grammy for her advice about my girl trouble. If my mother were alive, I'd ask her. But Grammy is so loving. I trust her. She knows something is wrong. She tilts her head and raises her eyebrows. That's my cue.

"Grammy, you're a woman."

She smiles.

"Well, what I mean is — why don't girls, or at least some girls, give boys a chance to explain when something weird happens?"

"What happened?"

"Well, two girls I like each think I'm dating the other one — even though I haven't actually gone on a date with either. But they won't let me explain. They just run away. Why won't they let me explain?"

Grammy rises from her chair, puts her hand on my shoulder, and tilts her head.

"I can't say for sure, honey," she says softly. "But it seems to me both of them are afraid you can't return their feelings."

"Yeah, you may be right."

"Give it some time," she adds, gently rubbing my back. "I'm sure they'll come around. And you might want to think about which girl you like best. As you can see, courting two girls often ends in heartbreak."

"Good point," I chuckle and give her a hug. I turn to go to my room.

"And, Bere," she pauses as I look back, "don't forget to look on the bright side."

"What's that?"

"How many times have two girls wanted you? Seems to me you've been doing something right."

"Yeah — yeah, you're right, Grammy. Thanks. I love you."

"I love you, too, honey. Sleep well."

My mood improves but I still feel sad. I don't like hurting people, especially those I really like.

*　*　*　*　*

I lock the door to my bedroom and insert the ziphoid drive into my MicroDell 3083. Ms. Gomez instructed me to give the drive to my dad, but she didn't tell me I couldn't look at it. A message pops up on my screen.

ENCRYPTED — LEVEL 8 — CLASSIFIED. PROPERTY OF THE CORPORATE DEPARTMENT OF DEFENSE. UNAUTHORIZED POSSESSION PUNISHABLE BY UP TO

Life in prison?

I'd better wait for Dad. I pull the drive out and put it into a secret compartment in my desk drawer.

I stay up until midnight.

But he's a no-show.

I fall asleep and wake at 3:22. I tiptoe into the garage to see if Dad's pod is there. It isn't. I send him a text. *When you coming home?*

No answer.

Strange. Dad has never gone anywhere without telling us where he is. Maybe he's in trouble. Maybe the ziphoid drive's got something to do with it.

I remove the drive from my drawer and insert it into my computer and give the "decrypt file" command. I hold my breath. The screen fills with numbers and letters as it searches billions of password combinations per second. A minute later it stops.

ENCRYPTION FAILURE. FILE REQUIRES MINIMUM OF
NOVEMDECILLION COMPUTATIONS PER SECOND.
DECRYPTION MAY TAKE 78 YEARS OR LONGER.

Holy moly! I'd be 94 years old.

I'm no computer whiz. Zach is. But should I get him involved?

I wake shortly after 8:30 and realize I didn't sleep well, but I've got to get going. I need to contact Zach. I don't need to tell him where I got the drive. I just need his help to decrypt it.

Grammy's in the kitchen. We exchange greetings and she says, "I still haven't heard from your dad. I'm going to the university to see if I can find him," she says, kissing my forehead. "I'll be back as soon as I can."

"I'll be at Zach's for a while," I say as she walks toward the door to the garage.

"Keep me posted as to your whereabouts."

"Will do, Grammy."

I text Zach, which woke him. *Sorry to wake you. Got a favor to ask. May I swing by?*

Of course, bro.

The air quality is low this morning — an atmospheric inversion, according to the weather service — so instead of walking I take Henry to Zach's house, which is a mile away. He lives with his mother, who's become a surrogate mom to me — next to Grammy, of course. Zach and I have attended the same schools since kindergarten, but only in third grade did we became close friends, when my mother died in a pod accident and Zach's father died in a chemical spill at work. Our tragedies bonded us.

I ring the doorbell and Zach's golden Labrador, Disco, greets me with a round of friendly barks from behind the door. Of course, he mobs me when Ms. Rodriguez opens the door, and I kneel and massage him with chest and belly rubs. "Have you been a good boy?" I rhetorically ask as he licks my hand and rubs his furry body against mine.

As usual, Ms. Rodriguez looks on and patiently waits her turn to address me after Disco runs back inside to get one of his toys. "Good morning, Bere," she says, hugging me. "Have you been a good boy, too?"

"Of course not, Ms. Rodriguez. I beat up a football player last night."

She laughs, assuming I'm joking. "You should leave those poor football players alone. Only pick on boys your own size."

"I wish I could, but almost all of the guys in my school are bigger than me."

She chuckles and shakes her head. "He's upstairs, in his room."

I climb the stairs and knock before entering Zach's bedroom.

"You may enter the inner sanctum if you have the correct passcode," he teasingly responds.

I play along and make one up: "Zach Rodriguez is the smartest programmer in the world."

"That's not the full passcode. You forgot to mention that I'm the best-looking programmer in the world, too. But I am a gracious man as well, so you may enter."

Zach's room is filled with black light posters; plastic models of planes, pods and vintage automobiles; long-play records from the 1960s and 1970s; and five holographic computer screens. I don't know how he can manage that many computers at once. I'm overwhelmed with just one screen.

"I am humbled by your majesty's presence." I say, to butter him up some more before putting him to work.

"Speaking of presence, where were you last night? Eleanor and I missed you."

"Sorry. Sara and Heidi met each other and both are mad at me. My love life is in the toilet right now. I'll tell you more shortly. First, can you — "

"Sara was at the party, too," Zach says, raising his eyebrows. "She asked me to tell you she's sorry — something about her accusing you of doing something that she was doing. You know what that means?"

"Yeah, I think so — I think it means I'm going to stay single all my life."

"So you won't mind if I make a move on Sara?"

"Hey, dude, you've already got a great girl."

"You're just jealous," he teases.

"Why would I be jealous? If you want to make a move on Sara, go ahead. I don't care."

"You can't fool me, bro. You like Sara. Come on. Admit it."

"Okay, okay, okay. I like her — as a friend, nothing more. She's got a boyfriend. End of story. Now can you help me decrypt this drive?"

"Only if you promise to invite me to your wedding."

"You're crazy." I push him off his bed and we wrestle on the floor until he's sitting on my chest and my hands are pinned.

"Come on, promise," he teases. "Promise."

"Okay, okay. I promise you'll be invited IF I ever marry. Now can we get down to business?"

He frees me. "Whatta ya need?"

"Can you decrypt this drive?" I ask, pulling the

device out of my pocket.

"What's on it?" he says, inserting it into a port.

"Don't know. But it's level 8."

"Wow, I've never decrypted anything above 6. Where'd you get it?"

I ignore his question, but when Zach sees the warning screen, he says: "Are you sure we should be looking at this?"

"To tell you the truth, no. But my dad's missing, and I'm supposed to give it to him. I'm thinking it might have something to do with his disappearance. Please don't say anything to anyone about this, including your mom."

"My lips are zipped."

For the next two hours Zach tries to crack the file, swiftly moving his hands from one screen to another and back to his keyboard. As his programs are running, we talk about school, our dreams and, of course, our girlfriends — or would-be girlfriends in my case.

"That's too bad about Heidi," he says. "But you've got Sara."

"I don't have anything yet. Sara was pretty mad at me."

"Eleanor has agreed to go steady with me," he says.

"Congrats, dude. That's wonderful. Gonna buy her a ring?"

"Of course, but this won't affect you and me."

"You mean we're still going steady, too?"

He laughs and adds: "I'm not gonna be a kept man, and Eleanor understands that. But maybe we can double-date."

"Of course — if I ever find a girl who isn't mad at me."

Zach tells me he wants to be a schoolteacher. Unlike me, he doesn't care to live in Partition 1. "A bunch of stuck-up people live there," he says. He's got a point. But the air is clean and it's safe.

"You'll make a damn good teacher," I say, lightly punching his shoulder.

"And you'll be a kind Vorster who will direct the Education Corporation of America and give me lots of raises."

"Only if you can decrypt this drive."

"Well, I'm sorry to say," he says, removing the drive and dropping it into my hand, "I'm going to be a teacher living in poverty. This is high-level encryption. But I've got a few online buddies who might be able to help."

"Let's hold off on that for now. I don't know where all of this is going, and I don't want to get anyone else in trouble."

"Okay, but I'll be there if you need me."

"You know you don't have to tell me that."

6

As Henry whisks me home, I want to call Sara. But I need to call my father first. "Call Dad," I say into my communicator, but the screen flashes and gives me an "out of service" message. I try again but it fails.

That's strange. I'll try the pod's communicator.

"Henry, call Dad."

No response.

"Henry, are you there?"

No response.

"Henry, switch to manual control of pod."

Still no response.

"Henry, what's going on?"

The pod's cover shield engages, blocking out the outside world.

"Henry, remove cover shield. Henry?"

Henry makes a sharp right turn, which causes the left side of my forehead to slam into the door's window, giving me a quarter-sized bump. Images of Henry crashing to the ground clog my thoughts. My body tingles, but not in a good way.

I pull a lever under the dash that releases a steering stick and floor pedals. I clutch the stick but it won't budge. My forehead is sweating.

Henry picks up speed, and I try to gain control of the pod but nothing works. The pod isn't falling, so that's reassuring. But I'm scared. I wonder if all of this is connected to the ziphoid drive, which is in my pocket.

Minutes later Henry slows and descends.

The door opens.

A man wearing a black ski mask points a microwave gun at me.

"Get out and gimme your communicator," he bellows.

A rush of adrenaline pulses through my chest. My knees feel weak. "What's going on? Where am I?"

"Shut up."

The man's voice seems familiar, but I can't place it. He has biceps the size of my thighs.

I step out of Henry into a desert peppered with bursage, scrubby mesquite trees, and wilting saguaros. He nudges me with the end of the gun and points at a dilapidated stone and wood building about two hundred feet in front of us. "That way."

I push a rusty metal door forward and enter the building. The ceiling is partially caved in. The windows are boarded up. It's dark, except for the dust-filled light from a small lantern on a wooden table. The room smells like a musty creosote bush, sweet and stale at the same time. A man wearing a mask is sitting on the edge of the table, in front of the lantern. He's older, with graying temples. I look around for a means of escape, but there appears to be only one door.

"Sit down," he commands. He points at a stain-faded oak chair near the table.

I can hear my heart pounding in my ears as I walk toward the chair and sit. Big Man holsters his weapon, folds his arms and stands in front of the door.

"What do you want?" I quietly ask. If they ask about it, I'll just say I found it in the school parking lot.

"Shut up."

My stomach churns like a cement bucket. I draw deep breaths in hopes they'll calm me.

"Where's your father?"

"Don't know. Haven't heard from him since yesterday morning."

The man bends over and glares into my eyes. I turn my head and grimace. His breath stinks. Sauerkraut.

"Have you ever thought of using a Cresgate laser tray?" I ask, wishing immediately that I could withdraw that question.

"I was told you're a wisecracker."

"Actually, smart-ass is more accurate."

He slaps my cheek.

"Ouch." I rub my face to erase the sting. Sara was right: I'm not good at negotiating with bullies.

"Quit your whining," the man barks. "You don't know what pain is." He raises his mask several inches to reveal a long deep scar on his right cheek. "Your Luminar friends did this."

"Sorry about your gash," I say with sincerity. "But I don't have any Luminar friends. I don't even know one. I hate Luminars."

"Bullshit. Your father's a Luminar, and you're going to tell me where he is."

"My father's not a Luminar!" I exclaim, stiffening my back. "He's a loyal American."

"Cut the crap. Where is he?"

"I don't know, and even if I did, I wouldn't tell you."

Scarface backhands me, knocking me onto the cracked concrete floor. I hate the smell of concrete. Blood oozes from the right corner of my lips and runs into my mouth.

I can't contain my anger. "Asshole!"

Scarface ignores the insult and walks toward Big Man. The two whisper. Big Man leaves the room. Scarface guards the door.

I stand and look again for a means of escape, but there's no other way out.

Big Man returns, jerking an elderly woman by the arm. Scarface walks behind me.

She stumbles. Big Man pitches her into another chair several feet in front of me. The lantern illuminates her face, which is covered with dried blood.

"Grammy," I gasp, jumping up, but Scarface pushes me down.

"I'm okay, honey," she groans. "Stay there."

Scarface pulls a handgun from the holster under his left arm. He screws a small cylinder onto the end of the muzzle — then pulls and releases the slide on the top of the gun.

CLICK, CLICK.

He points the gun at Grammy and stares at me.

"I'm going to make this simple, Bere. I'm going to ask you one more time for the location of your father. If you refuse, I'll shoot your grandmother."

"Bere doesn't know where his father is," Grammy interjects. "I don't know, either. Let him go. He doesn't know anything."

"Nice act, granny. But you're both lying."

Big Man kneels and pulls Grammy's arms behind her. Tears fill my eyes. This can't be happening.

Scarface points the pistol at her left bicep.

"Please — please don't shoot her," I plead. "I don't know where my dad is. That's the truth. Please don't shoot — "

A flash of light followed by a muffled CRACK!

Blood splatters onto Big Man's pants.

Grammy screams and Big Man releases her arms. She grips her upper arm to stop the bleeding.

"You son of a bitch!" I shout, lunging from my seat toward Scarface.

But Big Man blocks my path, pushing me back into the chair. "You're next, chink boy," he says, chuckling as he pulls my arms behind me.

"I recognize that voice — Otto, what the hell are you doing?"

"Shut up," Scarface says, pointing the gun at me.

My rage morphs into fear. I grit my teeth. This is gonna hurt, but if Grammy can take it, so can I.

"OK, granny, tell me where your son is or I'll shoot your grandson."

Grammy's eyes widen. Her right hand morphs into a fist.

"I don't know," she sternly shouts. "I'm telling the truth." Her eyebrows drop and her eyes narrow. "Please don't shoot Bere. He's just a boy. Please — "

I close my eyes.

SLAP! CRACK!

The gun fires, but I don't feel anything.

I open my eyes and for a brief moment wonder if I'm in a dream. Grammy's right palm is striking Scarface in the nose. He recoils, loses his balance and drops the gun as he falls back-first to the floor.

I blink several times. Did that really happen?

Otto releases me and rushes toward Grammy, but she pivots on her left leg and kicks him in the throat with her right foot. He stumbles back.

I jump out of my chair and kick him in the shin. He trips over the chair and lands on his back, coughing and grasping for air.

Grammy smiles and gives me a thumbs up as Scarface unexpectedly appears behind her.

"Grammy, behind you!"

She turns. Scarface swings his fist but she ducks, pivots and responds with a jab into his throat. She swings her leg behind him and kicks his leg out, pushing on his chest, which sends him slamming into the floor on his back.

"Bere, get the gun," Grammy yells.

I grab it and she points it at Scarface, who's moaning and coughing.

"Turn over on your stomach, shithead," she commands.

"Grammy," I exclaim. "Did you just call him a shithead?"

"Sorry, honey. I'll wash my mouth out with soap later."

"No apology necessary, Grammy."

Scarface moves his right arm and Grammy shouts, "Hands on the back of your head, feet out."

He obeys.

"You too, Otto," she says. "Bere, pull the microwave gun from his holster."

I hand her the M-gun and she gives me the pistol.

"Point the gun at Otto," she says.

"I've never shot a gun before. What if it accidentally goes off?"

"Just be sure it's pointed at one of them and not me."

I clumsily hold the gun with two hands My right index finger is on the trigger, but I hold it lightly. I've heard these triggers go off easily. My heart is pounding like a disco tune from one of Zach's long-play albums.

Grammy adjusts the settings on the M-gun and pulls the mask off Scarface. I recognize his face from the news yesterday. He led the raid on the Luminars.

"Well, well, well. If it isn't the infamous and ugly Colonel Wagner," she says. "So the TCP is making you do its dirty work?"

"Somebody's — gotta — clean house," he says, coughing between words.

"Like they say, nobody knows trash better than a dirt bag," she retorts.

"You know, we're going to catch and hang you."

"That's what the British said about the Patriots, and you know how that one turned out. Okay, why are you looking for Bryce?"

"That's a national security matter."

Grammy points the M-gun at Scarface's back.

Is she really going to shoot him?

She holds the trigger down for about three seconds and he screams as gun creates an intense burning sensation but nothing catches fire.

I wince.

"Torture me — all — you want," he says, trying to catch his breath. "I'm not going to talk."

"Okay, Colonel, your wish is my command," she says, giving him another burning jolt, this time for five seconds. He screams again, which makes me wince again, even though he kinda deserved it.

"Let's try the other trash man," she says, walking over to Otto. "Bere, point the gun at the Colonel." She removes Otto's mask.

"That's Otto Wagner," I interject. "He's on the high school football team — and let me guess, Colonel Wagner here is your pop. The apple doesn't fall far from the rotten tree, does it?"

Grammy kneels and pushes the nozzle of the gun into Otto's back. "Why are you and your father trying to find my son?"

"I don't know," he replies. "Dad doesn't tell me much. I'm just an assistant in training."

"And an asshole by nature," I add.

"Well, no need to waste any more time here," Grammy says. "I should kill both of you, but we don't believe in that. I'm just going to give you a good rest." She resets the M-gun.

"You're a softy, granny," the Colonel says. "That'll be your downfall."

"I prefer to think of myself as a humanitarian," she counters, zapping the Colonel, whose body goes limp.

"Is this going to hurt?" Otto whines.

"Not much as much as it should," Grammy says, pulling the trigger. She turns toward me. "They'll be asleep for about five hours. At least we know the authorities don't have your Dad."

I pass the handgun to her. "I think I know why they're looking for dad," I say.

"Tell me after we get out of here. Smash their communicators and yours."

"Do I have to smash mine?"

"Sorry, dear, they might track us."

"What about your arm, Grammy?"

"It's just a flesh wound."

I tear off a piece of my t-shirt and wrap her arm, which is soaked with blood.

"That's sweet of you, honey."

"You taught me well."

We leave the building and Grammy opens the door

to the Colonel's pod. She grabs an electronic device on the seat and shoots five bullets into the control board to disable it.

"I don't know where we are," she says. "But this jamming device will allow us to get back into Partition 2. We need to stop by the house."

"Why?"

"To pick up a few things."

"Are we going somewhere?"

"To safety," she replies.

"Shouldn't we report these guys to the authorities?"

"It's complicated, Bere. I'll explain later."

We climb into Henry.

"Grammy, the Colonel apparently used some device to control Henry, which is how I got here."

"They used this jamming modulator. I'll fix that."

As she fiddles with the device, I ask: "Grammy, where did you learn to fight like that?"

"There's a few things I haven't told you about myself, honey. I'll explain everything. First we have to get out of here." She passes her thumb over a screen on the modulator. "There, Henry should be fixed now."

"Henry, where are we?" she asks.

"Hello, Ms. Claire. We are in Vulture Mine, a ghost town about 45 miles northwest of Phoenix."

"Nice to see you're back, Henry," I say.

"Did I go somewhere?"

7

The sun is setting as Henry whisks us home at 80 mph — top speed for this pod model.

To the west, altocumulus clouds are saturated with layered sheets of orange and crimson. But their sedating effects are having no impact on me. I am filled with dread. Assaulting a police officer is a serious crime. How are we going to get out of this?

I have a zillion questions for Grammy. Why did the Colonel accuse my father of being a Luminar? Where did she learn to fight and use guns? Fix jamming devices? Who is this woman that I've known all my life?

But I'm too tired to grill Grammy right now. Adrenaline can do that to you, or so my science teacher said. So we're both sitting here, in the pod, thankful for the moment that no one is trying to shoot or chase us. Grammy looks at me and smiles awkwardly. She's trying to make me feel better, and it's helping. "Okay, honey," she finally says, "tell me why you think they are looking for your father."

"Before I came home last night, Ms. Gomez, my

government teacher, gave me this." I pull the ziphoid drive from my pocket and drop it into Grammy's hand. "She seemed frantic. She told me to give it to Dad — not to tell anyone. Sorry I didn't tell you earlier. I was trying to respect her wishes."

"I bet the Colonel thought your dad had it."

"What is it?"

She pauses and moans quietly.

"Does your arm hurt?" I ask.

"Just a little."

I think she's lying, but she returns to our conversation.

"I don't want to drag you into this any deeper, honey."

"I'm already in over my head, Grammy. I just helped you beat up a couple of police officers."

"And a good thing you did," she says, mustering a small smile. She pauses and looks out the window. "I suppose you're right. You're already in this. Okay, well, I don't know exactly what's on it, but rumor has it the drive contains sensitive information about the Trumpian Party of America. That's all I know."

"So maybe we should turn it over to the authorities."

"That might put your father in jeopardy." She clasps my hand.

"But isn't he already in jeopardy?"

"True, but this could make matters worse."

"How? Can't we turn it over and explain that it was all a mistake? They'll release Dad and everything is fine."

"It's not that simple, honey."

"Why not?"

"Because the information on that disk might save a lot of lives. I'll tell you more later. We're almost home and need to pack quickly. They're going to come after us when they find out what happened to the colonel and his son."

"Who's coming after us?"

"The bad guys, honey,"

*　*　*　*　*

The bad guys.

Are they the police?

A criminal syndicate?

Or a rogue operation inside the police or government?

I dismiss thoughts that my dad and Grammy are Luminars. After all, Dad's a respectable professor and Grammy — well, Grammy is Grammy: a loving woman who stepped in after Mom died. I don't know what I'd do without her. I'm confused right now. My mind swirls with questions, yet I'm not sure I want all of the answers. There's one thing I know I want: my life before this craziness.

Henry circles our home twice. "Looks safe," Grammy says. "Down, Henry."

"Fill a backpack with the essentials, honey," she says, as we rush into the house. "A change of clothes, toiletries, small valuables. Do you have any money?"

"Got some old silver and gold coins Dad has given

me through the years."

"Bring 'em. Okay, let's get moving. Five minutes."

I go straight to my room and quickly pack toiletries, a change of clothes, money, respirator, medicines. What else? Two minutes left. Calm down. We're coming back. I don't need to take everything. We can't abandon everything over a little ziphoid drive. That's crazy. On my bookshelf next to my bed is the teddy bear Grammy gave me when Mom died. I miss her. Why did she have to die?

"Bere?" Grammy calls out. "I'm in Dad's bedroom."

"Coming." Oh, what the hell. I grab the bear.

"Play security video 29A64X," she says as I enter the room. "You need to see this, honey."

The holograph begins with Dad sitting on the edge of his bed.

He's calm.

"Mom, Bere — if you're watching, it means I'm unable to contact you. Listen carefully. Go to the safe house in Anthem immediately. Henry and Mildred both have the location. You'll get further instructions there. Bere, sorry to put you in this spot. Grammy will explain. In the meantime, you'll need to see a man named Dale Greenstone, who works as a stockbroker at the Desert Plaza Tower on Central and Camelback. Don't call him. Wait for him in the Tower's parking garage, third floor, near the elevator, at 3 p.m. on any weekday. Playing this video has triggered a software program that will disable the security cameras in the garage between noon and 5 p.m. for the next five days. Dale will arrange to fake your death and will give you a new identity. It's the best way to keep you safe. But Dale won't help you unless you give him the passcode phrase, which is 'Man is born free, and everywhere he is in chains.' Memorize that phrase, Bere. 'Man is born free, and everywhere he is in chains.' I'm so very sorry this has happened. I'll get in touch as soon as I can. I love you both very much. Be safe."

"The passcode is a famous phrase from Jean-Jacques Rousseau," Grammy says.

"Who?"

"An 18th-century French philosopher. American schools no longer teach his ideas or the ideas of other philosophers of his time."

"Why?"

"Because those ideas challenge powerful elites who —— "

"No, I mean why do I have to take on a new identity? Can't I just be me? And what about my friends? My school? Our home? This is all crazy, Grammy. What's going on?"

"You aren't losing your life, honey."

"But Dad is saying I have to take on a new identity."

Grammy's deep brown eyes mist up. Mine were wetter.

"Honey, many of the things you've learned about America are just not true."

"Like what?"

"Like the fact that Luminars burned the White House down. They didn't."

"Who did, then?"

"Well, I — we — don't know, exactly."

"If you don't know, how do you know they didn't burn the White House down?"

"I wish I could explain everything right now, honey, but there just isn't time," Grammy says, looking out the window, "because they're here."

We hear the sound of broken glass coming from the kitchen.

She pushes a button behind an impressionist painting of a field of lavender on the wall of Dad's bedroom. We can hear the sound of gears turning as the foot of Dad's bed rises above our heads, revealing a set of stairs leading beneath the house.

"Holy shit," I exclaim.

"Follow me, and watch your language," she whispers.

I'm tempted to turn that command back on her. After all, she dropped more than a few cuss words when she was interrogating the Colonel and his son. But I know what she would say: "You can cuss all you want when you're eighteen."

At the bottom of the stairs, she opens a small panel cover on the wall and pushes a green button. The bed retracts as a thick metal door at the bottom of the stairs slams shut. Lights come on, revealing a tunnel constructed of concrete and steel. The walls are wide enough for two people to pass and the ceiling is higher than my outstretched arm.

Grammy punches several more buttons.

"What's all this?"

"Our escape." She starts running. "Do you think you

can keep pace with me, young man?"

I scoff and then realize that she's already 30 feet ahead of me. I run as fast as I can to catch up. I underestimate her again.

Moments later an explosive noise fills the tunnel behind us, followed by the sound of men's voices. The "bad guys" must have blown open the metal door to the tunnel.

"Faster, honey," Grammy says, picking up the pace.

We turn a corner, and she reaches out and pulls a red lever while still moving forward.

"Run like hell, honey."

She didn't need to explain.

Ten seconds later another explosion echoes behind us. I feel the rush of air from the blast and the sound of men screaming.

She signals with her hand to stop and listen.

We hear footsteps.

She reaches up and hits another red button.

"Run, run, run."

This time the blast knocks me down. She stops and helps me up. The tunnel and my lungs fill with dust. I can't stop coughing. Hard to believe this is happening. A tunnel beneath our home and Grammy is blowing it up. Crazy.

"Shh," Grammy says.

I muffle my cough.

We hear only the sound of a single set of footsteps.

"Damn," Grammy sighs. "You okay? The end of the tunnel isn't far."

I nod.

We run a couple hundred feet more, where we reach an elevator platform. She hits a blue button, then a red one. A thick metal mesh gate on the elevator closes in back of us. A red light in the ceiling flashes.

"Gotcha," a man's voice behind us says as the dust clears. He's dressed in black combat fatigues and is pointing a microwave pistol at Grammy, who's standing behind the mesh gate. I'm behind her.

"Please don't hurt my grandmother," I yell.

"I won't if she — "

His threat is drowned out by a recording: "This tunnel will self-destruct in one minute. Evacuate immediately. This is not a drill."

"Soldier, you can get to safety if you go back about twenty feet and go through the blue metal utility door."

He pulls the trigger on his pistol but it fails to fire.

"Microwave guns don't work down here," she says as the elevator begins to rise.

He wraps his fingers through the metal gate and is lifted as the elevator rises, but when the shaft narrows about 15 feet up, he releases his grip and falls to the ground.

"Quick — go through the utility door," Grammy shouts. "There's an escape hatch in there."

He disappears into the tunnel.

"Grammy, why did you try to save him when he just tried to shoot you?"

"He's just a victim, honey, like so many other people working for the TCP. They really don't know what's going on. We don't believe in killing unless it's absolutely necessary."

There's that "we" again. Who is we? Dad and her? Or other people, too?

The elevator slows and enters a large cave containing a matte black pod and a wall of electronics. Seconds later an explosion spews dust into the air near the elevator.

"I hope the soldier survived," I say.

"I'm sure he did," she says.

"What's all this stuff?"

"Our rainy-day fund." She reaches into a drawer. "Take this communicator. It's encrypted and will respond only to your voice or the iris of your eye. Keep it with you at all times. Your dad and I can always find you."

Grammy turns and faces the computer panel. "Charlie, this is Claire Baudin. Reveal weapon room."

"Voice confirmed," the computer responds. "Welcome back, Claire."

A two-inch-thick metal-plate door opens, revealing a cache of modern and conventional weapons.

"Wow!" I exclaim.

Grammy grabs a duffle bag and stuffs it with two microwave pistols, one rifle, two handguns, four vaporizing grenades, and five boxes of ammo. She picks up a what appears to be a grenade launcher.

"Is that what I think it is?" I ask.

"An old woman's best friend," she grins. "Honey, would you please put the bags in the pod?"

"I never argue with a woman holding a spatula or a

grenade launcher," I laugh nervously, still finding it hard to believe that she and Dad kept all of this hidden from me. Obviously they're part of some kind of secret operation. But Luminars are not known for being kind, so they can't belong to them. Grammy even refused to kill the Colonel and his son, and she helped that soldier escape. No Luminar would do that.

We stuff the weapons into the trunk of the pod and climb in.

"Mildred, this is Claire Baudin," she says.

"Identity confirmed," the pod's computer responds.

"Mildred?"

"She's no ordinary pod," Grammy says, activating the holographic control panel. "Stealth on."

"Stealth activated," Mildred replies, lifting off the ground a foot or two and hovering in place.

"Take us to the safe house in Anthem."

"Yes, Ms. Claire."

"What's Antum?" I ask.

"It's Anthem, as in a song. It was a suburb of Phoenix but abandoned during the civil war. Now it's part of Partition 3, where the Dregs live."

A metal wall in front of us retracts into the floor and Mildred zips out of the cave with a G-force that slams me back into the seat. I look back and watch as the outer wall, camouflaged with rocks and plants, closes. The cave was nestled in the western side of North Mountain. The sun is under the horizon but I can see our home, which is on the south side of the mountain, now engulfed in flames. I blink repeatedly to keep tears from running down my cheeks.

"I'm so sorry, Bere. Your dad and I never intended for this to happen. Your life and ours are going to change. But remember the most important thing: We love each other." She pauses. "Mildred, set cave self-destruct sequence for two seconds."

"Sequence set."

I watch as a massive fireball consumes the cave.

Mildred accelerates to 120 miles per hour and climbs to 5,000 feet, an altitude twice as high as Henry can fly.

Grammy and I are quiet on the flight to the safe house, which she said would take about 7 minutes. I try to imagine life without my home, my school, Zach, Heidi, and Sara. But I can't — it's like peeling away the layers of an onion, and there's nothing in the center.

Mildred slows and hovers in the twilight over a house on a cul-de-sac nestled between two hills. The area north of the home is open desert. The hills seclude the home from its two adjacent neighbors. The garage roof opens and Mildred descends.

"We're here," Grammy says, stating the obvious. "Don't leave the house, honey, especially at night. It's not safe."

Grammy leads me to a bedroom whose windows are covered with steel plates. I can't see out; no one can see in. "Clean sheets and blankets are in the closet, in a bag. Come to the kitchen after you're settled. I'll make us some dinner and we'll talk."

The bedroom is small and dark, with only three pieces of furniture: a bed, a nightstand and a lamp. The nightstand is covered with a layer of dust.

I'm worried about Dad. I hope he's safe. I pull "Teddy" from my backpack and put him on the bed. Memories of my mother flood my thoughts — the warmth of her hands, her smile, her hug. I feel like crying again, but I push thoughts of her out of my mind. I've learned how to do that to suppress the pain — except that, right now, this defense mechanism isn't working. I miss her so much.

*   *   *   *   *

I wipe my eyes and do my best to hide my emotions before making my way to the kitchen, where Grammy is preparing dinner.

"Hungry?" she asks.

"Starving."

"Good, because that's the only way these freeze-dried meals are going to taste good."

She smiles and stares into my eyes. "You okay, honey? I know the last 24 hours have been very stressful."

I nod.

She hugs me. I want to speak but I can't, because I'll start crying again. I should be stronger, but I just don't know how.

"There's no shame in crying," she says.

I burst into tears.

She tightens her grip. What would I do without her?

"I'm okay, Grammy." I grab a napkin off the table

and wipe my cheeks. "How's your arm?"

"No worse for the wear," she says. "I put some antibiotic cream on it at the house. Hardly any pain. Okay, let's eat."

She was right about the dinner. Tastes like cardboard. But I scarf it down.

"Okay, can you please tell me what's going on?" I ask. "How did you get your fighting skills? And why is the government — or whoever — chasing us?"

Grammy pushes her meal aside, takes a drink of bottled water, and folds her hands on the table.

"Okay, bear with me. I want to tell you the whole story, so you can understand what's happening. As you know, I was born in China and my father, Brad Baudin — your great-grandfather — adopted me and brought me to the states in 2001, when I was 16 months old. He was a loving man — very much like your dad. He worked as a professor and wrote extensively about the decline of civil liberties, due process, free speech, and democracy in America. ... "

I roll my eyes and slump in my chair as she continues talking. My great-grandfather sounds like a radical — like a Luminar.

"I could go on and on but my point is that I inherited his passion for freedom," Grammy says, unfolding her hands and scratching her forehead. "I worked as a lawyer, helping people who had been wrongly prosecuted or harmed by corporations or powerful people. I loved my job but was forced out of it after the Second Civil War. The only people who could practice law were those who signed a TCP loyalty oath. Well, I couldn't do that, so I took a job as a librarian and —— ”

"So are you saying," I interrupt, "that you and my great-granddad were — are — Luminars?”

"Give me a chance to explain, honey.”

"Was my mother one, too?”

"Just give me a chance to explain, please.”

I sigh and stare at the table.

"Before the war," she continues, "I met a man who was a historian. His name was Jonas. He and I married and we had your dad when I was 24. Several years later he was drafted into the army and was forced to work in a prison, where he executed people. He deserted and I hid him in the library basement. On the day before your father's eleventh birthday, Jonas went out to get some supplies, and the TCP arrested him. He was executed the following day, before he could even see your dad. It was a terrible time for me.”

"I'm so sorry to hear about that. Why didn't you tell me about this before?”

"Your father and I wanted to protect you. We probably should have told you sooner. I'm sorry about that. Anyway, after the war, the TCP ordered the library to burn tens of thousands of books. I saved about five thousand volumes, which I hid in a storage room in the basement the library. Those books are now —— ”

"Grammy," I interrupt, "are you a Luminar?”

She pauses and sighs. "Yes.”

"And Dad.”

"Yes.”

"And my mother?"

"Yes."

"So all of you are traitors?" I scream.

"Bere!" Grammy shouts and then lowers her voice. "There's a lot you don't know."

"I've heard all I need to hear," I yell, pushing my chair back, springing up. "How could all of you do this to me? My life is ruined. You destroyed my future!"

I rush toward the living room door.

She chases after me and gently touches my shoulder. I turn to face her. Her hands are cupping my upper arms.

"Bere, your future is not over. Your life has just begun, and it will be good again. I promise you."

Tears run down her cheeks.

But they have no effect on me. I break free and smash my palm against the two large deadbolts on the door, desperate to get away.

"Bere, please stay and let me explain."

"Don't touch me. I need to get out of here. I can't breathe."

"Bere, please — it's not what you think. Please!"

I charge into the darkness. No street lights. Just a sliver of a moon illuminating a landscape of hills and dilapidated homes. I run as a fast as I can down the street, which is strewn with burned out automobiles and debris.

"Bere, come back, please," she shouts from the doorway. "I'm sorry. Please come back. I'm so —— "

Grammy's voice fades as my legs carry me farther

from the safe house.

The Luminars destroyed this city. How could my family be part of this? I want my life back, my school, Zach. Maybe if I tell the police what happened, they'll understand. But what would they do to Grammy and Dad? What am I going to do? I can't ——

"OUCH," I scream, falling to the pavement.

My shin is searing with pain. It's bleeding; my elbows are skinned. I'm lying next to a rusty bicycle, trying to catch my breath. Wish I had my respirator. My leg pulses with sharp pains.

CLANG. CLANG.

I hold my breath and sit up. Voices. Dregs? Oh god!

I slowly rise and tiptoe back in the direction of the safe house.

"He's on the move," a man yells.

"I'm on it," shouts a woman.

I burst into a full run but moments later a net engulfs me and I collapse to the pavement. Can't move my arms.

"Got him," a woman screams, pushing her knee into my chest.

"Stop hurting me," I plead.

"Stop struggling," she shouts, covering my mouth and nose with her hands.

Moments later I see stars, but not the kind in the sky.

8

7:48 a.m., Sunday, December 16

I hear children shouting and laughing as cool air passes over my arms.

The sweet smell of alyssum fills my nostrils and reminds me of my mother, who planted and tended flowers in our backyard.

I open my eyes to a scene of a half dozen children playing soccer with a deflated ball in an open field that apparently used to be park, now surrounded by burned-out homes. Soccer is my favorite sport, but I confess I'm a mediocre player. I'm almost always assigned to play right fullback.

I feel a headache coming on, like the time I drank five shots of tequila at Zach's sixteenth birthday party. I'm outside, lying on a sofa under a corrugated tin roof held up by wooden posts. A gray blanket covers my torso and legs. My left shin aches. I look down at the desert floor and watch an Arizona bark scorpion scurrying away from the sofa, obviously more afraid of me than I of him.

I remember now — tripped over a bike — Dregs.

I sit up and discover my right leg is chained to one of the posts. I rub my eyes.

"Sorry I suffocated you last night," says a middle-aged woman to my left sitting in a rusty metal chair, the kind that used to populate backyards when Joe McCarthy charged that America was full of communists. She's wearing a tattered sweatshirt and jeans, but her face and hands are clean. "Didn't mean to black you out."

She apparently was seeking forgiveness. I didn't oblige. "Where am I?"

"You're in our camp. You're safe."

"If I'm safe, why is my leg chained?" I shake my leg to emphasize my point.

"Well, no one's gonna hurt you now."

"You in charge?"

"No, Jeremiah is. You'll meet him later."

"What do you want from me?"

"You'll have to ask him. Here's some water."

She hands me a red plastic coffee cup filled with a brown, cloudy liquid.

"You drink this?" I ask in disbelief.

"We ain't people of means, like you, rich boy," she scowls.

"My family isn't rich."

She rolls her eyes. "Yah, right. Whatta you doin' here?"

Before I can answer, a man swaggers toward us and says, "Okay, Sally, that's enough." He's tall, bearded, muscular — flanked by two other men who look like they were extras in a B-rated cartel movie. "Leave us."

Sally complies.

"So you're the one the fuzz is looking for," he says, pointing at me as he plops down into the chair. He spits.

"Am I?"

"That's what the news says."

"Are you Jeremiah?"

"I am, and you're Bere Baudin — the high school kid who's a Luminar."

"I'm not a Luminar. Why does everyone keep saying that?"

"Who's everyone?"

I ignore his question. "Who are you?"

"Sally already told you. I'm the leader of this here tribe. The Blackrocks." He points to a hillside behind the soccer field, which is filled with basalt stones.

"Where's the others?"

"They're in a village, a short distance from here."

"Why am I chained?"

"Insurance. You're worth a lot of dough."

"My family doesn't have any money."

"But the TCP does. They're gonna give us $2 million for you and your granny. Where is she?"

"I don't know," I say, looking at the ground, afraid my eyes will reveal my lie.

"We can do this the easy way or the painful way," he says, leaning forward in his chair. "Your choice."

"My choice is for you to let me go. I can assure you my grandmother is not a woman to be trifled with."

Jeremiah leans his head back and belly laughs.

"Ha, ha. I like you, kid. You got spunk. But yur gonna tell us where she is. Sebastian, show him."

Sebastian, a scraggly man with an unkempt goatee, pulls a nightstick out of his belt and begins slapping it slowly in his left hand.

A wave of adrenaline washes through my body.

Jeremiah leans forward. "Okay, where's your granny?"

"I don't know. We had an argument and I ran away."

"Where were you when you had the argument?"

"I don't remember. It was dark."

"Sebastian," Jeremiah says. "Help him remember?" Sebastian grabs my right arm, pulls it out, and lays his stick on it.

"One last time, where's your granny?"

"I'm right here, Jerry," a voice floats in from an area filled with browning palo verde trees and bursage.

Sebastian releases my arm, and Jeremiah leaps out of his chair. Both hit the ground and stare at the terrain behind me.

"Stay right where you are, Jerry. I've got an TZ-8 pointed right between your eyes. If you move or anyone comes near me, you'll be the first to get a splitting headache."

Sally yells at the children to get off the playground and run behind a concrete bunker.

I give Jeremiah a smug grin. "I warned you."

He ignores me and shouts: "All right, granny. We ain't gonna to do nothing to your grandbaby. Why don't you come down here so we can talk?"

"I'm comfortable where I am, Jerry. In fact, I could sit here all day with you in my sights, although my trigger finger is twitching right now. But I'm in a good mood today, Jerry. I'm willing to spare your life if you'll have Sally remove the chain from my grandson's leg and if you thank us."

"Thank youz? For what?"

"For saving your life — twice."

"What?" He looks around but still cannot locate Grammy.

"You getting senile, Jerry?

"Whatta you talkin' about?"

"Angela saved your life about ten years ago in Prescott."

"Yeah, I remember. But what's that got to do with your grandbaby?"

"Angela was his mother."

"His mother?"

"Yeah, Jerry — Angela Baudin."

My mother saved Jeremiah?

"So you must be Claire Baudin, the radical attorney. I remember you. Why didn't you say so earlier?" Jeremiah turns his head to look for Sally, who heard the conversation and approaches him. "Sally, remove Bere's leg iron. My apologies. Come on in."

Jerry stands up.

"How can I trust you, Jerry?"

"The police will be here in about five minutes. Would I have told you that if I were lying?"

Grammy emerges from a thick stand of creosote

bushes, keeping her rifle trained on Jeremiah as she walks toward me. She's carrying the grenade launcher, which is strapped to her back. "There isn't time enough to get the pod here," Grammy says.

"Sally," Jeremiah says, "take them into the butte tunnel. I'll stall the pigs."

"We appreciate this, Jerry," Grammy says.

"I'm the one who's indebted," he says, turning from Grammy to look at me. "Your mother was the bravest woman I've ever known. Now get out of here, or we'll all be jail mates."

I'm craving to hear more details of my mother's heroism, but Sally is waving for us to hurry.

We follow and enter a dirt tunnel hidden by rusted pipes, pieces of corrugated metal and old tires. Railroad ties hold back the earth on the walls and ceiling. We duck to make our passage. A few minutes later we push some bursage out of the way and emerge on the north side of the butte. A white-tailed rabbit scurries behind a jumping cholla cactus. In the distance are small mountain ranges, mostly dark shades of brown and patches of green, made up of palo verde and mesquite trees.

"Mildred, come to my location immediately," Grammy says into her communicator.

"You won't be safe here for long," Sally says. "The drones and cops will come over the ridge in a couple of minutes."

"Thanks, Sally," Grammy says, looking up at the butte's ridge. She removes the grenade launcher from her back, opens its sights, pulls back the slide to insert a large blue-tipped grenade, and snaps it back into place. "When they come over the ridge, I'll be ready for them."

"Don't judge Jeremiah too harshly," Sally says. "He got a soft side, too. He was just thinkin' 'bout the tribe. We don't have much."

"We understand. We'll be back some day. Go now, so you don't get caught up in this."

Sally disappears into the tunnel, and seconds later two mini-copter drones appear at the top of the butte.

"Bere, when the pod arrives, get in. I'll be right behind you."

"Grammy, I'm so sorry. I should have listened to you. This is all my fault."

"No harm done, honey." She smiles. "You've got every right to be angry. Your dad and I kept you in the dark to protect you. We should have told you sooner."

"This is the second time you've saved my life, Grammy."

"Bere, your dad and I give thanks every day for the joy you've added to our lives. Don't you dare blame yourself for anything." She looks to the east. "Here comes Mildred."

As the pod descends, surveillance drones come over the ridge and hover in place.

I climb into Mildred.

Grammy comes over, reaches into her pocket and drops the ziphoid drive into my hand. "Please get this to your dad. Lives depend upon it." She looks up. Two police officers emerge at the ridge. "Here come the bad guys.”

“Grammy, come on — get in.”

She ignores my comment and points the grenade launcher at the right side of butte, away from the officers’ location. She pulls the trigger and the grenade shoots out of the tube, striking in front of a large boulder. The blast sends pieces of dirt and shrapnel flying into the air, obscuring the view of the officers.

“Leave, Bere,” she says, positioning herself behind a large boulder and firing another grenade far short of the top of the ridge to obscure the officers’ view.

“I can’t leave without you,” I yell, motioning with my arms to come to the pod.

“Mildred, leave immediately and enter stealth mode 9.”

“No!” I scream, but the door slams shut and the pod turns and lifts off the ground as several bullets from the officers’ guns glance off its bulletproof shell.

“Go back, Mildred,” I yell.

“Sorry, Mr. Bere. Ms. Claire programmed me to override your commands until we get to a safe location.”

I look back just as Grammy drops her launcher and raises her hands into the air to surrender.

9

1:03 a.m., Monday, December 17

"Bere, wake up," Mildred says. "WAKE UP!"

"Okay, okay," I grumble, wiping my crusty eyes. "What time is it?"

"1:03 a.m., Monday, Dec. 17, 2059."

"Are you kidding me?"

"No, I am not programmed to jest. You are thinking of Model 347, which was manufactured in —— "

"Okay, okay — got it. So I slept for 12 hours?"

"Twelve hours, 36 minutes and 10 seconds. You are a teenager, and teenagers require 15 percent more sleep than adults."

"Thanks for the details," I say irritatedly.

"You're welcome."

"Where are we?"

"In a cave in the McDowell Mountains east of Scottsdale. Ms. Claire programmed me to take you to a safe place after the raid and to wake you when there is news of your father."

"So what's the news?"

"The police have arrested him and charged you with

murder."

"What?" I screech. "Murder? Who did I kill?"

"Jeremiah. You mean you didn't?"

"Of course not. Is there a news story?"

"Yes, here's the TCP wire service story."

ARIZONA CORPORATE POLICE ARE SEARCHING FOR A 16-YEAR-OLD PHOENIX BOY WHO SHOT AND KILLED A DREG LEADER SATURDAY IN THE CITY FORMERLY KNOWN AS ANTHEM.

POLICE SAY BERE BAUDIN, A KNOWN LUMINAR, MURDERED JEREMIAH ARROWHEAD IN COLD BLOOD. BAUDIN IS 5-FOOT-7, THIN, CAUCASIAN AND PART CHINESE, AND IS CONSIDERED DANGEROUS.

HE IS THE SON OF BRYCE BAUDIN, A LUMINAR WHO WAS ARRESTED TONIGHT FOR AIDING AND ABETTING LUMINARS AFTER A RAID THURSDAY NIGHT ON THE MOGOLLON RIM. ...

"Those sons a bitches!" I scream.

"Your grandmother would not approve of your language, sir."

"Mildred, I think this situation is worthy of an exception."

I pull the ziphoid drive from my pocket and stare out the window for several minutes, thinking about how to make things right.

"Mildred, you still in stealth mode?"

"Yes."

"Can we go back to the safe house?"

"No, the corporate police are there."

"Okay, plot a course to Zach Rodriguez's house on Palm Court Lane."

"Are you sure that's wise, sir? The police are probably there. They know he's your friend."

"Well, if I ask him to meet me somewhere, I put him in more jeopardy. He'll be an accomplice. Hey, how is it that you can ask your own questions?"

"Remember when Ms. Claire told you I was special? I'm the newest generation of synthetic artificial intelligence computers made in South Sudan. I have the ability to make probability generalizations, but I lack the capacity to understand emotions or humor."

"That isn't always a shortcoming, Mildred."

"Can you clarify what you mean, Bere?"

"Later. We've got more pressing matters."

I send Zach an encrypted text message: *You up? Coming over.*

I'm up, but the cops are watching the house. Your picture is all over the news. They say you killed the leader of a Dreg group.

That's a lie.

You didn't have to defend yourself to me, bro.

I need your help. I'll be there in 10 minutes.

Minutes later Mildred hovers three blocks from Zach's home.

"Mr. Bere, my scanners show at least four police officers are outside Zach's house."

"Thanks, Mildred. Set us down in that parking lot below."

"May I suggest that you don the stealth suit? It's in the trunk."

"You may, Mildred. Didn't know Grammy had one."

"She never leaves home without it."

"I guess there's a lot I don't know about Grammy."

"She earned three black belts in the martial arts. She can hit a six-inch target a mile away with the .50-caliber rifle. She can —— "

"Tell me more later, Mildred. See you in 45 minutes. If I don't return, go back to the cave and wait for me to contact you."

"Yes, Mr. Bere."

The suit covers my entire body and includes night vision goggles. I activate them, insert my respirator, and run as fast as I can. Two officers sitting in a police pod in the front of Zach's home look directly at me but do not respond. The suit is working.

I climb the six-foot-high cinder block fence in the backyard of a home half a block from Zach's house. I walk on its four-inch-wide concrete ledge, holding my arms out to keep my balance.

Zach's dog Disco smells me and barks. My heart skips a beat but returns to normal when three or four other dogs start barking, which masks my location.

I climb a metal trellis to reach the second story of Zach's home and slide his bedroom window open. I've done this many times before. I remove the suit's hood.

"Hey bro," he whispers, "where'd you get the stealth suit?"

"From Grammy's wardrobe."

"I thought it was a little big on top," he says.

"Hey, that's my Grammy you're talking about," I scold. The grin on his face disappears. "If the cops break in here," I add, "you tell 'em I was trying to steal some of your stuff and that you didn't know I was a Luminar."

"You're a Luminar?"

"No, well, maybe yes. It's getting complicated, and the less you know the better off you are. Just tell the authorities that you have no knowledge of what I am doing and what I'm going to ask you. Second, you don't have to help me, and I won't be offended. Just my being here is putting you and your mom in jeopardy, but if I asked you to meet me somewhere else, that would even be worse. You don't have to help me."

"Bro, why are you even saying that? You're hurting my heart."

"Don't make me cry, dude. I've already done that enough today."

"I'm assuming all of this is related to the ziphoid drive?"

"Good deduction, bro. Did the cops talk to you?"

"Yeah, but I didn't say anything about the drive and told them I hadn't seen you since Friday night. By the way, Eleanor said Sara asked about you again. She wants to talk to you."

"I had intentions of calling her today, but my schedule has been a bit busy."

Zach smiles and lightly punches me in the stomach. "Hey, she likes you, dude."

"When I get out of prison fifty years from now, you

think she'll still be waiting for me?"

Zach chuckles. "Maybe not, but I'll be there to pick you up."

"Great. We can swap incontinence stories. Here's the ziphoid drive. Can you copy this?"

He pauses and scratches his head. "If the file on the drive is the original encrypted file, no. But if it's a copy, yes."

"I'm guessing this file is a copy, since it's a portable device."

"How long will it take?"

"A couple of hours," Zach says, popping the drive into his system.

"Text me when you're done. I'll give you a location to drop off the original drive."

*　*　*　*　*

Five minutes later I climb back into Mildred for the return trip to the McDowell Mountain cave.

"Wake me when Zach texts, but no later than 9 a.m."

But I can't sleep. I keep thinking about Dad and Grammy. Are they being mistreated, tortured? Will the TCP kill them? How could they and my mother be Luminars? Yet how could I have been a Trumper? They falsely accused me of murder! That's like something right out of a movie. I was taught that Trump and his followers always told the truth. Elections were stolen. Fact. And that's one of the reasons they were banned. The other is that most people are too ignorant to choose their leaders. Only the smartest have the right to rule. Even Plato made that argument, according to Ms. Gomez.

But right now politics seems insignificant when compared to my family. I can't imagine life without my dad and Grammy. It's been so hard since Mom died. Mom. I miss her. And there's a lot I don't know about her. How and why did she save Jerry? Will I ever learn the truth?

I look up into the moonlit sky and I see a pack of buzzards circling. I didn't know they flew at night. I look down and see Grammy and Dad standing on the edge of the Grand Canyon. What are they doing there? *Don't walk back,* I yell out. I reach out to pull them from the edge, but they fall, because I pushed them. Why did I do that? Heidi and Sara appear and begin yelling at me and each other. The two girls morph into an image of Zach, who smiles and then turns into a two-headed monster, one of which says: *Do you know what you're doing, bro?* The other responds, *No, he killed his grandmother and father.* The heads laugh and then swoop down, opening wide to consume —

"Bere, wake up," Mildred says. "Zach texted."

My shirt is soaked in sweat. "What time is it?"

"8:25."

Success, Zach says in the message. *Attached is the copied file.*

You're a genius, dude, I respond. *And good looking, too.*

LOL.

I laugh and text back: *Now, please put the original drive in a small waterproof snack back. Get some fresh dog poop from your back yard, and smush that snack bag into the middle of the poop and put the entire load into a sandwich-sized bag. Put that bag in your pocket and take Disco on a walk to the park. When he dumps a load, pick up the poop in a sandwich-sized bag and put it into the pocket of your jacket. Walk to the garbage bin at the entrance to the park and throw the poop bag with the ziphoid drive into it.*

Now you really owe me big time, bro, he responds.

I doo-doo.

Zach posts a laughing emoji.

The cops undoubtedly will follow you to the park, I add, *but they aren't going to open a bag of shit and check it.*

Let's hope you're right.

Zach, one more thing: Don't believe everything you hear on the news tonight, okay?

Hey, I don't believe anything on the news. After all, it comes from the TCP.

A day ago I would have disagreed with him. I feel so foolish about the way I treated Kiryn. *Text me when you drop the load.*

Forty minutes later Zach responds. "You were right, bro. The cops looked in the garbage but didn't pull out the bag."

"It may be a while before I see you again, Zach. I'm going to miss you and your mom."

"Same here, bro. Take care of yourself and your

family."

"Mildred, let's go," I command. "First, to pick up the doo-doo and then to the Desert Plaza Tower parking garage."

Mildred and I arrive at the parking garage fifteen minutes before 3. The garage is full of pods, but only one man is walking toward the elevator.

I don a hooded windbreaker I found in the trunk. "Mildred, I'll be back in an hour or less. You know what to do if I don't return."

My heart is pounding again. I look down to reduce the risk of someone recognizing me.

I reach the elevator and meet with Mr. Greenstone. We talk for about a half hour and agree to meet again at 5 p.m. in the basement of a building in downtown Phoenix near the Walter Cronkite School of Corporate Journalism.

10

On my way back to Mildred I can't help but fret over whether the plan will work and how strange all of this is. Three days ago I was a typical high school student, hoping for a date, and now I'm a fugitive from the law trying to find a way to save my family. I want to call Sara, but I don't have time for that.

I climb into Mildred and place a video call on my personal communicator to TCP headquarters in Phoenix.

"May I please speak to Col. Wagner? Tell him this is Bere Baudin — killer of women and children."

The receptionist sighs at my sarcastic attempt at humor. "One moment please."

My hands are shaking, so I drop them below the visual area of the screen. During the pause, the video switches to a TCP newscast. "In national news — Gebieter John Kaiser has announced the passage of a new law that makes it a crime to associate with a known Luminar. Violators will face up to forty years in prison or banishment to Partition 3. All citizens must report any known Luminars to the authorities within —— ”

“You did the right thing by calling me, Bere,” the Colonel says, leaning back in his chair behind his desk. “I can help you. Where are you?”

“I’d like to make a deal, Colonel. I’ll turn myself in if you release my grandmother and father.”

“How noble of you, Bere. But I don’t care about you. All I want is the ziphoid drive. I know you have it. Give it to me now and I’ll quash the warrant for your arrest.”

“Release my family and I’ll give you the drive.”

“I’ll release your father, but not your grandmother until I get the drive.”

“If I give you the drive, how do I know you’ll release her?”

“You don’t have a choice, kid. If you don’t turn over the drive, both of them will be executed. Where are you?”

“Release my father immediately and drop all charges against him. Report this on the TCP network. I’ll call you back when I see it on the news and when you put my father on the call. Then I’ll give you a meeting time and place.”

“All right, I’ll do it. Don’t forget to call back.”

“How could I forget you, Colonel?”

*　*　*　*　*

Twenty minutes later TCP News broadcasts a report saying that all charges against Professor Bryce Baudin have been dropped.

I call the Colonel. Dad is standing next to him.

"Bere, you okay?" Dad asks. His lip is cut and there's some blood on his shirt.

"Fine, Dad. Are you okay?"

"Don't worry about me. You should see the guy who tried to arrest me."

In that moment I could see where I got some of my sense of humor.

"Grammy and I were worried. Just to make sure it's you, I have a question for you: What did Grammy give me after Mom died?"

"A teddy bear."

"They have Grammy."

"I didn't know that." He purses his upper lip and stares at the Colonel.

"All's fair in love and war, professor," the Colonel shrugs. "You're an academic — you know that."

"What I do know is that if you hurt her," Dad says, raising his fist, "I'm coming for you, Colonel."

The Colonel laughs. "Now, now, now. Let's not get violent, professor. We're here to do business, not to seek retribution."

"Colonel," I interrupt, "in two minutes a pod will arrive outside of your station. That pod will take my father to a safe location. The pod has tracking sensors that can detect radar or objects tracking it. If it detects anything, the deal is off."

"Don't you worry about a thing, kid," the Colonel says. "We won't tail your dad."

"I hope you know what you're doing, Bere," Dad says.

"Trust me, Dad. Call me from the pod's communicator when you're safe. Colonel, I'll meet you at the Cronkite School of Corporate Journalism in downtown Phoenix at 6 o'clock. Bring my grandmother. If you fail to bring her, the deal is off. I'll give you the ziphoid drive after I know my grandmother is safe."

"But," shouts my Dad, "the TCP will never —— "

"Don't worry," the Colonel says, cutting him off. "We'll bring your grandmother. Just make sure you bring the drive."

About ten minutes later, Dad calls me from the McDowell Mountain cave.

"I'm safe, Bere. Where are you? What are you going to do?"

"I'm in downtown Phoenix. Greenstone is preparing to kill me."

"Be careful, son. I love you."

"Love you, too, Dad," I say, wiping a tear from my eye.

11

5:50 p.m., Alley Next to
Cronkite School of Corporate Journalism

I take a Luber to the Cronkite School and now I'm standing on a sanitary sewer cover in an alley south of the building, watching twilight turn to dusk. The six-story building houses the studios of the TCP National News Network and trains all of the journalists who work at local TCP stations throughout the nation. From where I stand, I can see Space Park, to the west across Central Avenue, where a pod will whisk Grammy to my father.

The Colonel is late.

I begin to worry that he's up to something devious.

But my fears are allayed when a black pod descends and parks on the west side of Central about a hundred feet in front of me. The Colonel emerges and walks to the passenger side of the pod and opens the door. My grandmother, who is handcuffed, steps out. Both of them walk toward me and cross Central. Grammy looks okay.

Four students walking on the sidewalk stop and give the three of us bewildered glances. Three journalists burst out of the front door of the Cronkite Building and begin filming the scene. Greenstone tipped them off.

"That's far enough, Colonel," I say, when they're on the sidewalk, about 60 feet away. "Everyone else, stay back. Are you okay, Grammy?"

"I'm fine, honey," she says, "with the exception of this asshole standing next to me. You okay?"

"I confess I'd be doing a little better if the asshole next to you hadn't falsely accused me of murder."

Grammy cracks a smile. "I normally would chastise you, honey, for using a cuss word, but in this case the appellation is a good fit."

The Colonel cocks his head to the side. "Okay, enough chit-chat. As soon as you give me the drive, I'll release her."

"Let her go now," I shout. "Grammy, there's a pod in the park behind you. Get in. It's pre-programmed."

"I'm not leaving without you, honey."

"Grammy, it's my turn to give the orders. Please trust me."

"I do, and for once, your granny is going to keep her mouth shut. But don't count on that happening often."

I chuckle.

The Colonel removes Grammy's handcuffs. She jogs toward the pod.

"Okay, Bere, I've given you what you want," the Colonel says, opening his hands in a sweeping motion. "Now give me the drive."

"Not until Grammy is safe."

She enters the pod, which lifts off the ground and

speeds away.

Grammy calls me on the pod's communicator. "Everything looks fine, honey. I don't see any police pods. Now get out of there."

"I've upheld my end of the bargain," the Colonel shouts. "Where's the drive?"

I pause to give Grammy a little more time to get away. "It's in the potted plant to the left of where you're standing."

He quickly retrieves the drive and plugs it into his communicator. He nods and mumbles something.

Seconds later, a half dozen men in dark gray combat fatigues emerge from the Cronkite Building and point assault rifles at me. The civilians run for cover across the street. My communicator buzzes.

"Bere, the pod's descending," Grammy says. "I'm surrounded by police. Get out now —" The transmission abruptly ends.

"You lying bastard," I shout at the Colonel as I remove a vaporizing hand grenade from my coat pocket and pull the pin. "Stay back."

"Hold your positions," the Colonel commands the soldiers. "Bere, put the pin back in that grenade."

"Where I come from, the truth means something, Colonel."

"You are so naive, kid. People lie all the time. Parents lie to kids. Leaders lie to their followers. Trump lied about the election fraud. Welcome to the real world. The only thing that really matters is money and power. And you, your father and grandmother have none. You're all losers.”

“And you believe you and your son are winners? You’re just minions, doing the dirty work of powerful megalomaniacs. They don’t care about you.”

“Yeah, but they pay well. I’d rather be rich than loved.”

“And that’s where you and I differ, Colonel. Love is more precious than money. You’d know that if you loved anything.”

“Love all you want. You and your family will hang from the gallows.”

“You’re wrong, Colonel. You’re the one who’s going die today.”

I release the safety lever on the grenade and swing my arm, but the explosive slips out of my hand onto the pavement next to me.

“Oh, shit!” I scream.

“Hit the ground!” Wagner shouts, and the officers comply.

I turn to run but am too late. The blast creates a 10-foot-deep crater and vaporizes everything within a 30-foot radius — including the holographic projection camera set up in the storm sewer beneath the manhole cover on which my projection was standing.

* * * * *

“Congratulations, Bere — you’re dead,” Greenstone says as I step down from a filming platform located in a building a block away. “Superb performance. And now you get a new identity — a new life. What would you like to be called?”

I hadn't even given it a thought. All I could think about was Grammy. "What will they do to her?”

"They won't kill her," Greenstone says as he packs up the equipment. "She's too valuable. They know she's someone important. The tunnel leading from your house to the cave gave that one away.”

"So what's her role in the Luminars?”

"You don't know? She's president, the leader.”

"President? I had no idea.”

"Neither do the police, at least at this point in time. Your grandmother is a remarkable woman. The most honorable and courageous person I've ever known. I'm sure I don't have to tell you that.”

"No, but it's my fault she's still in custody.”

"Bere, no plan can control for every contingency. You did your best. Besides, the Luminar leadership team urged her for years to move to a safer location. But she insisted on living in the belly of the beast, where she thought she could do the most good. She knew the risks. Right now she's more worried about you than herself.”

"Well, I won't stop worrying until she's free.”

"Don't worry, the organization will come up with a plan.”

"With my help.”

"I'm sure there's something you can do," Greenstone says, packing up the holographic control board. "It's a good thing your grandmother brought some vaporizing grenades from the cave. We could have never pulled this off.”

“And what role does my dad play in the Luminars?”

“He’s chief of intelligence. The ziphoid drive was supposed to be delivered to him, not you. But Friday morning he was helping people who escaped in the Mogollon Rim raid.”

“What’s your role in the organization?”

“I’m known as Lazarus. I help Luminars start new lives by killing off their old ones. By the way, the copy of the ziphoid drive you gave me is now in the hands of the Luminar leadership. How did Zach pull that one off?”

“He exploited a flaw in the anti-copy encryption software.”

“You know, he could be a valuable asset to our organization.”

“Please don’t ruin his life.”

“We won’t. I promise. But we’re going to provide some surveillance protection for him and his mother, just in case. Unfortunately, I have some more bad news for you. The police executed Ms. Gomez.”

“Oh, my god,” I moan. I sit on a chair next to the platform and put my head in my hands. “How could they do that? Those fricking monsters. She was a wonderful teacher. And I acted like an idiot on the last day of school in her class.”

“We don’t know what she told the cops. But we do know she never told them she gave you the drive. That’s why the cops were looking for your dad.”

“How could I have been so blind to all of this?”

“Because your father and grandmother wanted to

protect you. One slip of the tongue on your part and all of you could have been spending the rest of your lives in prison."

"No, I mean, how could I have been so blind to the horrible deeds by the cops and the TCP?"

"Because Trumpians suppress a lot of information and quickly arrest people who challenge them. That's why the drive is so important. It allegedly contains a lot of info about the TCP and its history — stuff that is supposed to be very incriminating. You and Zach may have saved many lives. In fact, you're heroes."

"I sure don't feel like one. I feel like a failure."

"Do you think Martin Luther King Jr. always felt like a success?"

"Who?"

"Sorry, forgot your classes no longer discuss the good deeds of great civil rights leaders. He was the most famous civil rights leader in American history. He felt like a failure just before he was assassinated in 1968."

"I guess there's a lot I don't know about this country."

"It's not your fault. Through the ages, elites in all places and times have manipulated the masses. Power flows from the top down. It's always been that way, and likely always be, though hopefully less so one day."

Greenstone packs in a power cord and closes the holographic case. "Are you ready to go? We need to get you and your dad out of the country ASAP. The cops are going to create one of the biggest dragnets in history for him."

*   *   *   *   *

Greenstone's decision to fake my death outside of the TCP National News Network was brilliant. The event was broadcast live and very convincing. The broadcaster's script filled in the details.

A 16-YEAR-OLD LUMINAR WHO MURDERED A DREG LEADER AND ELUDED AUTHORITIES FOR TWO DAYS ACCIDENTALLY KILLED HIMSELF MONDAY NIGHT IN DOWNTOWN PHOENIX.

BERE BAUDIN DIED WHEN A VAPORIZING GRENADE HE ATTEMPTED TO THROW AT ARIZONA CORPORATE POLICE SLIPPED OUT OF HIS HAND AND EXPLODED. THE BLAST CREATED A 30-FOOT-WIDE CRATER.

NO POLICE WERE INJURED.

A DAY EARLIER BAUDIN WAS CHARGED WITH SHOOTING TO DEATH JEREMIAH ARROWHEAD, A DREG LEADER WHO LIVED IN DISTRICT 3 NEAR THE FORMER CITY OF ANTHEM.

BAUDIN'S GRANDMOTHER, CLAIRE BAUDIN, WAS CHARGED WITH ATTEMPTED MURDER FOR SHOOTING AT POLICE AS HER GRANDSON ESCAPED FROM ANTHEM. SHE IS IN POLICE CUSTODY.

AN ARREST WARRANT HAS BEEN ISSUED FOR BERE'S FATHER, BRYCE BAUDIN, WHO ASSISTED LUMINARS EVADING CAPTURE AFTER A RAID ON THE MOGOLLON RIM AREA THURSDAY NIGHT.

SECURITY POLICE COLONEL MAX WAGNER SAID

Bere's death should serve as a lesson to all young people: "Don't associate with or help Luminars. They are a grave threat to the security of our great nation."

As Greenstone's pod shuttles us to my father, I try to come to grips with the fact that "Bere Baudin" and his dreams are over. He would never become a Vorster and live in Partition 1. He was vaporized on December 17, 2059 — at least ... that's what the official record will show.

(To Be Continued)

Young Adult Dystopian Novel Targets Trumptocracy

PHOENIX — Can a teenage boy and his friends save America from Trumptocracy?

That's the central question addressed in a controversial new dystopian novel series for young adults that, according to its author, "seeks not only to entertain but to awaken" them to the dangers that Donald Trump's ideas pose to democracy.

"The Killing of Bere Baudin portrays life four decades from now, in an America that has replaced democracy with Trumptocracy, an autocratic form of government," said author David Demers, a mass media sociologist and former newspaper reporter whose passion for free speech and civil liberties often got him into trouble but sparked a landmark federal appeals court ruling that extended constitutional protection to faculty speech uttered outside of the classroom (*Demers v. Austin*, Ninth Circuit Court of

The Killing of Bere Baudin is the first book in the Luminar Papers series. The book explores what life would be like if Donald Trump's followers seized power.

Appeals, 2014).

"A lot of news stories and commentaries today lay bare the dangers that Trumpian and radical right ideas pose to democracy, free speech, civil rights and civil liberties. My goal is to show Americans what life would be like if most of these ideas were actually enacted. I chose young people as the target audience for the book, because they are the ones who would be living under these policies."

The novel begins in the year 2059 — 24 years after the "Second American Civil War."

> "Big themes, strong characters, skillful world-building, suspenseful story-telling, witty dialogue, and even a dash of romance — [*The Killing of Bere Baudin*] checked all of the key boxes for me."
>
> *– Elizabeth Bruce*
> *Senior Editor, Kevin Anderson & Associates, New York City*

Donald Trump is long gone, but his followers have seized power and have abolished voting, civil rights and civil liberties. Schools have purged pro-democratic ideas from their curriculums. Protestors are executed, jailed, or forced to live in Partition 3 with the Dregs.

"A dictator called the Giebeter and 27 privately owned corporations control everything, including schools, government, police, and courts," Demers explained. "Everything is privatized. There is no 'public', no voting, no free press, no due process, few environmental protections."

Yet many citizens embrace Trumptocracy, including 16-year-old Bere Baudin, who aspires to be a wealthy Vorster and live in Partition 1, a domed city with fresh air. His dreams are shattered, though, when one of his teachers gives him an encrypted ziphoid drive to give to his father, who has disappeared.

Police search for Bryce Baudin and arrest Bere and his grandmother. They escape, but Bere becomes distraught after learning that his father and grandmother are both Luminars, an outlawed group seeking to restore democracy. When police falsely charge Bere with murder and arrest his father and "Grammy," he embarks on a mission to free them and uncover the mystery of the encrypted drive. But first he must convince Mr. Greenstone to help him.

> *"What can I do for you, Mr. Baudin?"*
>
> *My heart is pounding so hard I can feel it in the tips of my fingers.*
>
> *I take a deep breath. "I — I want you to kill me."*
>
> *Greenstone stiffens his posture. ... "I'm sorry. ... I'm a stockbroker, not a killer. But I can refer you to a good therapist." ...*
>
> *I lean toward Greenstone and whisper in his ear, "'Man is born free, and everywhere he is in chains.' Now will you kill me?"* (Excerpted from Chapter 1)

Although *The Killing of Bere Baudin* is a work of fiction, the notion that the United States or other democracies could embrace autocratic forms of rule is no longer in the exclusive realm of science fiction, Demers said. Freedom House — a nonpartisan, nonprofit organization — has documented a 7 percent decline in democratic processes from January 2017 to January 2021, when Trump occupied the White House. More than two dozen countries around the world now have stronger protection for democratic processes and freedom than the United States.

"This book is not a prediction of what will come," Demers writes in a note in the front of his novel, "but a warning of what could happen if Americans fail to defend democratic processes, civil liberties and due process."

Demers said he expects some Trump supporters and conservatives to criticize the book. "I welcome the criticism and encourage them to write their own novels about the future of America. Let's see whose vision is more appealing."

The Killing of Bere Baudin is the first book in the Luminar Papers series and is loosely based on the 1971 Pentagon Papers case, in which the Supreme Court prohibited the Nixon Administration from censoring publication of a secret history of U.S. involvement in Vietnam and southeast Asia.

The novel will be available for purchase on April 1, 2022, through Amazon, Barnes & Noble, and bookstores. Ingram and Baker & Taylor are distributing the book.

A card game based on the book also will be available ($10.95; UPC 195893475506) from Amazon or directly from Marquette Books. The game is patterned in part after rules in rummy and poker.

Demers worked as a newspaper reporter, market research analyst, and professor before taking early retirement from Washington State University. He is author

The Luminars Card Game uses a 54-card full-color laminated deck and can be played with 2 to 4 players (average playing time 40 minutes for four players; 25 for two).

or editor of 18 trade and academic books, including *Adventures of a Quixotic Professor: How One Man's Lifelong Passion for Social Justice Bristles Bureaucracies and Sparks a Landmark Free Speech Ruling* (2021), which chronicles personal and social history of *Demers v. Austin* (Ninth Circuit, 2014), a federal lawsuit that forced WSU administrators to stop punishing faculty for on-the-job faculty speech critical of administrators and their policies. Demers can be reached at david@luminars.org.

An electronic copy of this news release with full-color photographs is available at

https://marquettebooks.com

Also, visit https://www.Luminars.org for updates on the Luminar Papers series

The Killing of Bere Baudin
By David Demers
116 pp, 5 x 8 format
Paperback $14.95 • ISBN 978-1-7327197-8-1
E-book/Kindle $2.99 • ISBN 978-1-7327197-7-4
The Luminars Card Game $10.95

Marquette Books LLC
16421 N. 31st Ave., Phoenix, AZ 85053
509-290-9240 (voice and text)
https://MarquetteBooks.com
books@marquettebooks.com

https://www.Luminars.org

www.ingramcontent.com/pod-product-compliance
Lightning Source LLC
Chambersburg PA
CBHW021737190726
48288CB00009B/3088